MERGER & SUBMISSION

A BDSM Office Romance Novella

APRIL CROSS

CONTENTS

Author's Note

Hey,

Before you dive into Maya and Gabriel's story, I wanted to take a moment to share something with you. This book contains references to a character who lost her mother to cancer. These mentions aren't graphic or extensive, but they do inform Maya's background and motivations.

This element of the story is personal to me. Having lost my own mother to cancer, I understand how unexpectedly encountering this topic in fiction can sometimes catch us off guard, especially if we're simply looking for a sexy escape.

I believe in giving you this information upfront so you can decide if this is the right time for you to read this particular story. The references are handled with care, but I know that sometimes our hearts need different things on different days.

Thank you for spending time with these characters. I hope their journey brings you joy, heat, and maybe even a few moments where you need to fan yourself!

April

CHAPTER 1

The lights flicker overhead, casting shadows across the grimy floor, somehow making the empty subway car more ominous after my long day of classes and work in Midtown. My legs ache from standing through my coffee shop shift that just ended. Only two more weeks of classes, and then once I graduate, I can find something full time and ditch my two jobs.

I clutch my backpack more tightly as the door at the far end opens and a man walks on. He's tall, broad shouldered, mid-to-late thirties, probably smells like money and orgasms. His suit is charcoal gray and perfectly tailored with fabric that screams *I charge more per hour than your rent.*

I look once—a quick glance, totally casual—and then immediately pretend the gum on the floor is fascinating because holy shit, he's gorgeous. And powerful-looking. And way too polished to be on this train with the rest of us plebs.

I mean, seriously? What is this man doing here? Did his town car explode? Did his driver quit? Is he doing some sort of a "slumming it for empathy" millionaire challenge? Shouldn't he be somewhere with a private elevator and a bottle of scotch that costs more than my student loans?

When I risk another glance just to confirm he's real and not a hallucination, our eyes meet. It's not a glance, it's a collision. My skin prickles, and suddenly, it's hard to breathe.

The way he looks at me is not polite or casual. It's like I'm already naked and he's deciding what to do with me. Like he knows things. Sinful, toe-curling things.

Nope, not interested. Not at all. I'm just...appreciating the aesthetic. Like art.

A very fuckable painting in motion.

Yeah, okay. He's hot. Fine. He's stupid hot. And the worst part? He definitely knows it. That's the look a man gives when he's used to getting exactly what he wants. And right now, apparently, that's eye-fucking me.

"You shouldn't be alone in an empty car," he says.

His deep voice makes heat pool between my legs while my brain wars with my body. Is he serious? And is he warning me or threatening me?

I search his face, trying to read his intentions while pressing my thighs together and praying I'm not drooling over a psycho. This could turn into a horror movie so quickly. Like one of those "woman disappears on subway" headlines in the news.

"The other cars are packed." I grip the metal pole next to me and mentally catalog potential weapons in my backpack. Economics textbook? It's heavy enough to do damage.

"It's safer with more people around." He moves closer. The spice of his cologne hits me, and my body goes haywire while my nipples tighten beneath my thin t-shirt.

I should leave and find another car like he suggested, but my feet stay rooted to the spot.

"I can handle myself." I aim for confidence, but I can hear the tremor in my voice.

A ghost of a smile touches his lips, and something hot and liquid pools between my legs.

He grabs the pole just above my hand, caging me without touching. "Can you? What's your name?"

Fuck. This shouldn't be turning me on. He's a stranger, possibly dangerous, definitely presumptuous. But my body disagrees violently with my brain.

"Maya," I answer truthfully, and then wince. Why am I giving this guy my real name?

"Maya," he repeats. "I'm Gabriel."

The train jerks suddenly, lurching forward as we leave Grand Central. I stumble, and he catches my waist with his free hand, steadying me. The warmth of his palm burns through my t-shirt while he spreads his fingers against my side.

My head spins. I've never reacted this strongly to a stranger, and I'm not sure I like it. My body has clearly never heard of stranger danger.

"Careful," he murmurs.

He doesn't remove his hand even though I'm stable, and being this close to him makes my body tingle all over. I should pull away and tell this creep to stop touching me, but something about him makes me want to lean into his touch.

"Thank you," I whisper.

His fingers tighten slightly, a squeeze that sends electricity through me. "Where're you headed, Maya?"

The way he says my name makes my thighs clench. I'm soaked already—from what? A hand on my waist and a commanding tone? Clearly, it's been way too long since I've had sex. I've been busy going to school during the day and working nights after breaking up with my last boyfriend two years ago. I haven't had time to date anyone.

"East Village," I say, not specifying further. No need to mention my illegal basement studio where the hot water works three days a week if I'm lucky. Better than flooding, I suppose. Which totally has happened before.

He nods toward my backpack. "Student?"

"Double major in Business Administration and Legal Studies," I reply. "I'm finishing up in two weeks."

Something changes in his expression. Interest, maybe approval. "Ambitious."

"Necessity," I correct, then flush. Why am I telling him anything? I guess I'm just a slut who enjoys attention from hot, rich guys, even creepy ones.

Except my instincts aren't screaming danger, unless the danger is my soon-to-be-ruined panties.

"And what do you do?" I ask quickly, redirecting my thoughts.

"I work at a law firm. Reed & Associates." He releases my waist, and I have to steady myself so I don't sway towards him.

My heart skips a beat. They're one of the top corporate firms in the city. It's the type of place I used to dream about working at before reality forced me to downgrade my expectations.

"Reed & Associates?" I repeat, trying to sound casual and failing miserably. "I actually interned at Jackson & Klein last year before I had to—"

I stop myself before admitting I had to quit to take service jobs that paid actual money. That internship had been the best three months of my life until everything changed. When my mom was diagnosed with cancer, our world shifted overnight. Between the treatments and mounting medical bills, I had to make an impossible choice. I said goodbye to my dream job and hello to coffee stains and customer complaints, trading legal briefs for whatever work would pay the bills while we fought her battle together. Even after I lost her, the financial reality remained

He assesses me with an intensity that makes me feel naked. "We should continue this conversation over coffee."

Not a question. A statement. The assumption that I'll agree sends another pulse of heat through me.

"Should we?" I challenge, even as my body screams yes.

He reaches into his jacket, produces a business card, and places it in my hand. "Call this number when you reach your stop. I'll send a car."

Jesus Christ, who does this? And why am I considering it? I check his left hand for a ring. Nope, doesn't have one. Not that it guarantees anything.

"I don't know you." Captain Obvious, reporting for duty.

"But you want to."

I should be offended. Instead, it's the hottest thing I've heard in years.

The train slows as we approach Union Square, where crowds wait on the platform. He steps back, giving me space I don't want.

"Your choice, Maya. The car will wait thirty minutes."

He exits before I can respond. Through the window, I watch him stride across the platform, people moving out of his way.

I stare at the embossed card. Gabriel Reed, Managing Partner, Reed & Associates Law. The paper is thick, expensive, and the address is in one of those fancy Financial District towers.

I should throw this away. I absolutely should not call this number. This is how women end up on true crime podcasts.

But...

My fingers trace the embossed lettering. Managing Partner. At Reed & Associates. A connection like this could change my career trajectory. Two years of serving lattes and cramming for exams, all to get my foot in exactly this kind of door. And now it's being handed to me by a man who makes my panties wet just by existing.

Is it worth the risk? Meeting a stranger for what's obviously not just coffee? My practical side says hell no, but my ambitious side whispers that opportunities like this don't come along every day. And the part of me that hasn't been touched in two years is screaming for me to call the damn number already.

I pull out my phone once I exit one stop later at Astor Place. The street bustles with its usual mix of students, tourists, service workers, and trust fund hipsters. The thought of weaving through the mostly drunk crowds for blocks on my sore feet appeals even less than usual.

Shit, fine, okay. I tap the number into my phone and hit call before I can talk myself out of it.

I'm calling because the look in his eyes promised something I didn't know I needed, my career could use the boost, and for the first time in forever, my body is desperate for whatever he's offering.

Just please don't let him be a psycho.

CHAPTER 2

The phone barely rings once.

"Maya," Gabriel answers. It's not a question—he knew I'd call.

"I'm at the station," I say, trying to sound casual but hearing the breathlessness in my voice.

"The black Audi S8 outside. Ten minutes." He disconnects.

What the hell am I doing? Meeting a stranger who barks orders at me? My pussy throbs at the thought, answering before my brain can.

Yep, this is definitely why I need therapy. But therapy costs money I don't have, so tonight I'm making another questionable life choice and meeting this guy for...coffee? Sex? A murder plot? Who knows?

I push through the crowd, October wind whipping my chestnut hair across my face as I spot the sleek black Audi. The driver steps out, and he's wearing a dark suit, earpiece, the works.

"Ms. Maya?" he asks, opening the rear door.

If this was a movie, I'd be tossing popcorn at the screen and yelling for the woman to run. Instead, I'm sliding into the backseat. The car pulls away before I've settled, gliding into traffic with a purr.

"Where are we going?" I ask, running my fingers over the hand-stitched armrest and trying not to think about how many double shifts it would take to pay for just this door panel.

"Mr. Reed's private office in the Obsidian Tower," the driver answers.

My stomach flips. Not a coffee shop. The Obsidian Tower is what the news calls "the billionaire's playground."

The car weaves through traffic, the Financial District growing brighter as we leave my familiar East Village behind. We pull into an underground garage beneath a gleaming skyscraper. The driver escorts me to a private elevator, scans a keycard, and steps back.

"Top floor," he says as the doors close. "Reed & Associates occupies the upper five levels."

Oooh, swanky. I catch my reflection in the mirrored walls. My cheeks are flushed, my hazel eyes too bright, and I'm wearing my best thrift-shop jeans and t-shirt that suddenly feel like a Halloween costume. I look exactly like what I am: a broke college student who is turned on and trying to hide it.

The elevator opens into a stunning office. Floor-to-ceiling windows frame the city skyline, lights twinkling below. Gabriel stands at the window, still in that impeccable suit, looking out at his domain. His reflection shows him adjusting a platinum cufflink. Is that a nervous habit or power move?

"You came," he says, turning to face me.

"I did." My voice sounds steadier than I feel, and my legs tremble slightly as I step onto what's probably a hand-woven Persian rug.

His eyes rove over me in a slow assessment and my nipples harden beneath my shirt. I'm suddenly aware of how my budget-friendly clothes must look to someone who probably has a closet bigger than my entire apartment.

He moves to a sideboard where crystal decanters catch the light. "Drink?"

"No." I need all my wits about me. "Thank you," I add, my mom's voice in my head reminding me about manners.

He pours himself something amber and takes a sip. "Why did you come?"

"You're the one who invited me."

He moves closer, stopping a few feet away. His cologne, woodsy and expensive, reaches me. "That doesn't answer my question. Why did you accept?"

"Curiosity," I manage. I wish he'd just do whatever he brought me here to do, and hopefully it's something sexual so I can tell all my future friends about the crazy night I hooked up with some rich dude.

"Liar." His voice is soft but certain.

"Excuse me?" Hmm, he might be an ass, but my body hums with electricity just being near him. Maybe I can hate-fuck him and leave satisfied without wanting to see him again.

"You're not here out of curiosity." Another step closer. "You're here because something unexpected happened on the subway." His steel-blue eyes hold mine, unwavering, like he can see every dirty thought in my head.

I back up until I hit his desk. It's a massive, gleaming mahogany surface that looks perfect for him to bend me over. "I don't know what you mean."

"Yes, you do. Your pupils dilated when I touched you, and your breath quickened. Your pulse"—he reaches out, fingers brushing the side of my neck—"jumped. Just like now."

I'm unable to look away, and I have to fight the urge to lean into his touch. "That's just—"

"Attraction. Primal and immediate," he finishes, tracing my jawline with his finger. "The question is what to do about it."

My pussy buzzes with neediness, making clear thinking impossible. I should tell him to fuck off and that he's going to have to give himself a sad hand job because I'm not attracted to him. But there's no point in lying. He knows I want him. And if he told me to kneel and suck his cock right now, I'd do it and then thank him after.

"Tell me to stop," he murmurs, his face inches from mine.

I say nothing. My body already decided back on the subway that it wanted to ride this red-flag express train straight to disaster.

His lips brush against mine softly, as if he's testing me. I stay still, afraid if I move, I'll grab him and try to swallow him whole.

"I have a proposition for you," he says against my mouth.

Mmm, yeah. I bet he does. And I'd like to RSVP *hell yes.*

"I'm listening," I whisper.

He steps back, breaking contact. The loss feels like someone yanked away a warm blanket. His jaw tightens as he puts distance between us, like he's fighting his own instincts.

"I need a personal assistant." He adjusts his cufflink again. "Someone intelligent, discreet, and willing to learn. Come work for me after you graduate."

Wait, what? A job offer? Not where I thought this was going. I'd been preparing for him to bend me over his desk.

"You don't know anything about me," I point out, trying to hide my disappointment that the proposition didn't include me riding his cock to glory.

"I know what you're studying. I know you work to pay for school, and the calluses on your hands tell me it involves manual labor. I know you respond to authority." He nods toward my worn backpack. "And I know you need money."

His ability to read me so easily should offend me. Instead, I'm intrigued. And even more turned on. I do need money since my student loans are massive and I've been working two jobs just to stay afloat since Mom died, but I really want his cock inside me more.

"What would this job entail?"

"Professional duties during business hours...and whatever develops between us after hours."

Oooh, bingo. I might get ravished on his desk, after all.

"That sounds like a sexual harassment lawsuit waiting to happen," I say, the legal studies part of my brain kicking in despite my arousal.

He laughs. It's a genuine laugh that transforms his face and makes him look younger. "Which is why you'd sign a Waiver and Release of Liability. Nothing happens you don't explicitly consent to." His expression grows serious. "I don't take what isn't freely given."

A job at a top firm would be incredible for my career. The salary alone would eliminate my financial stress. And the other part...

"Why me? There must be a hundred women better qualified. Women from your world."

"Because your body responded to me before your mind could object. Because you called, despite knowing better. Because you're still here when any sensible woman would have left. And because I don't want someone from my world."

Fuck, fuck, fuck. He's right. About all of it.

"Think about it." He moves back to his desk and pulls a folder from the drawer. "The job description, salary, and expectations are all here. Including a confidentiality agreement regarding any personal arrangement."

He's done this before. I feel like that should repel me, but it doesn't. It just means he knows what he's doing.

"And if I'm not interested in the personal aspect?" I ask, still lying to myself.

"The job offer stands." He hands me the folder. "But we both know that's not why you called."

I take it, our fingers brushing. Even that small contact sends electricity up my arm. The salary figure on the cover sheet makes my eyes widen. It's triple what both my current jobs pay combined. That's more money than I've ever seen. That's pay-off-student-loans-and-actually-eat-real-food money.

"What happened to the last assistant?" I ask, suddenly wondering if I'm just the newest in a line of girls he's fucked and discarded.

His jaw tightens. "She's now the head of our pro bono department." He meets my eyes directly. "I reward loyalty and competence. In all areas."

Well, shit. Not what I expected.

"You have until the end of tomorrow to decide." He moves behind his desk, signaling our meeting is ending. "Jackie, my executive assistant, will expect your call. She's the only one who knows about these arrangements."

Just like that, I'm dismissed. His attitude should annoy me, but I'm a turned on, wet mess instead.

"I'll let you know tomorrow," I say, clutching the folder.

The desire in his gaze nearly melts my panties. "I look forward to your answer."

The driver is waiting for me down in the garage. As we glide through late-night Manhattan, I flip through the folder. The "personal expectations" section makes my cheeks burn.

> The undersigned (hereinafter "the Submissive") expressly and willingly surrenders authority over specified aspects of personal autonomy to the Dominant during agreed-upon intervals. This surrender constitutes a devotional act, not of inferiority, but of profound trust and mutual fulfillment. Control shall be exercised within predefined parameters, with the Dominant assuming responsibility for the Submissive's wellbeing within these boundaries. This dynamic extends beyond the physical into psychological territory, wherein the Submissive finds liberation through structured service and the Dominant derives fulfillment through meticulous stewardship.
>
> **Implementation Framework**
> a) **Discreet Behavioral Modifications:** Adherence to

covert directives during professional engagements (e.g. , wearing specified undergarments without visible indication, subtle physiological responses to private commands in public settings).

b) **Sensory Management:** Controlled exposure to stimuli using approved workplace implements (e.g., temporary blindfolding with silk ties during private dictation, auditory restriction via noise-canceling earbuds keyed to the Dominant's voice channel during focused tasks, calibrated discomfort from seated positions maintained for negotiated durations).

c) **Possessive Marking:** Authorization for non-permanent, concealable demarcations of ownership (e.g., discreet symbols penned beneath clothing, temporary jewelry indicating the Dominant's preference in metal against skin).

The undersigned acknowledges that any physical relationship will involve power exchange dynamics, including but not limited to dominance/submission roles, with clear safe words established (red/yellow/green) and regular consent check-ins

I stare at the words until they blur. The contract specifies penalties for noncompliance—not legal ones, but intimate forfeitures that tighten my throat. I'm a wreck by the time the driver drops me at my apartment. My practical side screams this is insane, but I've already decided.

Hell yes, I'm taking that job. More money than I've ever dreamed of and a chance at his cock. Win/win.

I toss and turn all night, dreaming of Gabriel's hands on me, his voice ordering me onto my knees, his approval when I please him.

I'm still aroused when I wake up, and I desperately hope I'm not signing up for the world's hottest cautionary tale.

Chapter 3

Two weeks later, I stride through the revolving doors of Reed & Associates, my heels clicking confidently against the marble floor. The pencil skirt and silk blouse I'm wearing are treasured finds from my thrift store hunts. They're professional enough for a prestigious law firm but fitted enough to remind Gabriel what awaits after hours. Building a suitable wardrobe for this place devoured a chunk of my savings, but with my college degree finally in hand and a position at one of the city's top corporate law firms, every penny feels worth it.

The lobby reeks of money—leather furniture, fresh flowers, and whatever fancy cleaning products rich people use. I approach the security desk where a guard checks my ID. As I wait for my temporary access card, I feel a pang of loneliness. I'd texted my coffee shop manager Kristy last night about my first day at a prestigious law firm, and she sent back a quick "Get it girl!" with party emojis. It was nice but highlighted how superficial most of my relationships were. When Mom was sick, I dropped out of my social circles, and afterward, working two jobs while finishing school left no time to rebuild those connections. I haven't had anyone to really talk to about any of this since I don't have a best friend to call with excited screams or warnings about red flags. It's just me, making decisions alone, like always.

"First day, Ms. Williams?" The guard jolts me back to the present as he hands me a temporary access card.

"Is it that obvious?" I smooth my skirt, wondering if my thrift-store accessories scream "poor girl" despite my careful outfit selection.

He smiles. "Everyone looks a little overwhelmed on their first day."

Great. I'm already broadcasting "doesn't belong" vibes. I clutch my cheap leather portfolio tighter and head to the executive elevator. I remember the last time I rode it to meet Gabriel. Hell, I've been touching myself for two weeks thinking about what he might do to me. I'm so worked up I might come if he just gives me one command. But my body needs to slow down. I'm sure he won't do anything to me on the first day.

The elevator shoots up forty-five floors in seconds. When the doors open, I smell freshly brewed coffee, not the burnt sludge from the diner where I used to work.

I still can't believe I'm here. I'm walking into a top law firm as a personal assistant to one of the most powerful attorneys in the city. If only my mom could see me now, landing a proper job with benefits and everything right out of college. I just hope I don't fuck it up by being too distracted by Gabriel's...everything.

"Good morning, Maya." Gabriel's voice hits me before I fully exit the elevator. He stands in his office doorway, perfect in a navy suit. His eyes scan me with the same intensity from our first meeting, making my nipples harden instantly.

"Good morning, Mr. Reed." I'm proud of how steady I sound despite my fluttering stomach.

"Your desk." He points to a sleek workstation positioned to monitor his office. "Your orientation packet is waiting. The confidentiality agreement is on top."

I nod, unsure which role I'm playing right now. Am I his assistant or is this whatever we're becoming after hours.

We move into his office, and he closes the door behind us before activating the privacy screen. The glass walls turn opaque, shutting us off from the rest of the firm.

"Coffee first," he states, and I realize there's a kitchenette tucked in the corner. The espresso machine looks like it could launch a rocket to Mars.

I follow, watching the way he moves. There's no wasted motion. Everything in his office screams money and power. The carpet's so thick my heels sink with each step. It's a very different universe from what I'm used to.

He hands me a cup, deliberately brushing my fingers. I try not to react to his touch, even though it feels like that small contact has already branded me. The cup is bone china, so delicate I might crush it with my waitressing-strong grip.

He watches me over his cup. "Do you plan to sign?"

"Sign what?" I ask, playing dumb. I take a sip of coffee to hide my nervousness and nearly moan at how delicious it is. This is what coffee should taste like. It's not the watered-down stuff I've been serving for years.

"The personal arrangement." His eyes lock on mine. "The job is yours, regardless."

My pulse races. "I'm here, aren't I?"

He sets his cup down. "That's not an answer. I need absolute clarity."

My brain is like mush, and I almost joke and tell him he can use whatever hole he wants, but I glance toward the still-open door. This is a professional environment despite our conversation, and I can't be caught telling my boss that he can fuck all my holes.

"Perhaps we should close the door for this discussion," he says, moving to shut it.

My hands tremble as I set down my cup next to the espresso machine. "I'm interested in both aspects of the position. But I need to understand exactly what that means."

"Smart," he says, approval in his tone. "During business hours, you're my personal assistant. You'll work directly with me on specific matters, manage my calendar, prepare for meetings, handle correspondence, and learn the business. Jackie is my executive assistant who handles the general business of the firm. You'll be paid exceptionally well and evaluated solely on merit."

I nod, relieved by the clarity but impatient for the rest.

"After hours," he continues, his voice dropping, "I want your submission. Complete and willing. I'll push your boundaries but never break them. You'll have safe words—red for stop, yellow for slow down, green for continue. I'll never do anything that causes genuine distress or harm."

My body lights up. This directness is terrifying and arousing. But I'm curious what he thinks the benefits are to me, other than his cock. "And in return?"

His lips quirk. "In return, you get pleasure, growth, and experiences few will ever know." He steps close enough that I can smell his cologne again. "And my attention. When we're together, nothing else exists for me but your responses."

Fuck, my legs feel weak. I don't know this man, but I want everything he's offering. This might be the worst decision of my 26 years, but it doesn't matter. I'm going to let him do whatever he wants to me.

"Your first task is simple," he says in that commanding tone that makes my body respond instantly. "Take off your panties."

"What?" I glance at the clock, and it's barely 8:45 a.m. I didn't expect my panties to come off this quickly.

"You heard me. Consider it your first act of trust."

Here? Now? Where someone could walk in?

"The privacy screen is closed," he adds, reading my hesitation.

My heart pounds against my ribs. This is a prestigious firm. I can't walk around without panties, can I?

"Really?" I ask, my voice embarrassingly breathy.

"Now." No room for negotiation.

I bite my lip, weighing options. This job could change my life—financially, professionally. And this man...God, he makes me wet just by existing in the same space.

"It's your choice," he reminds me. "Always your choice."

That does it. The control he gives me is by reminding me I have it.

I reach under my skirt, hooking my thumbs in my cotton panties. They're nothing fancy, just clean and practical. When I dressed this morning, I really didn't think I'd be showing them to him today, let alone removing them in a corner office forty-five floors above Manhattan.

The fabric slides down my thighs as my face burns. I step out of them, wobbling slightly on the plush carpet. Gabriel's only visible reaction is his jaw tightening.

"Hand them to me," he says roughly.

Jesus Christ.

I pick them up, and the plain cotton dangles from my fingers. I really should have worn something nicer. If I'd known this was going to happen, I would have spent my last twenty bucks on something lacy instead of on ramen and peanut butter.

He tucks them into the pocket in his slacks. The thought of my panties against him, hidden beneath that expensive fabric while he conducts business, makes my pussy throb.

"Good," he says simply. "Your orientation begins now. I have a client meeting in two hours. You'll take notes and learn how this office operates."

Just like that, it's back to business.

"Yes, sir," I respond automatically, the word slipping out.

His eyes flash. "Sir. I like that. Use it when we're alone."

The air between us crackles as I murmur, "Yes, sir," again.

"Go review your packet and sign the paperwork," he says. "I also need you to understand the Morrison account basics before the meeting."

I nod, turning to leave, acutely aware of the air against my bare skin beneath my skirt. My body tingles at the thought of sitting through a meeting with no panties while trying to be professional.

"Maya."

His voice stops me at the door.

"You'll excel at both aspects of your job," he says. Not a request or prediction. A command.

The throbbing between my legs intensifies. "Yes, sir."

At my desk, I can feel Gabriel watching through the glass partition as I sign the documents that give official consent to him to dom me. I cross my legs carefully, mindful of the wetness already gathering. I click my pen nervously as I read through the legal jargon, a habit my mom always told me was annoying. The thought of her makes me pause. Would she be proud of me for landing this job or worried about the strings attached? Both, probably.

Once I'm done signing, I go back to the Morrison account files. They're complex—corporate restructuring with international implications. I should be intimidated. Instead, my mind works with surprising clarity, as if the arousal sharpens my focus rather than dulls it. My color-coded notes start filling the margins as I organize the information in a way that makes sense to me.

"Maya." A woman's voice startles me. I look up to find an elegant woman in her fifties standing before my desk, silver-streaked hair in a perfect chignon. "I'm Jackie Remington, Mr. Reed's executive assistant."

"Nice to meet you," I say, rising to shake her hand. The movement sends awareness rushing through me. I'm meeting coworkers while wearing no panties at my boss's command. My cheeks flush.

"Everything all right, dear?" Jackie asks, eyes shrewd behind designer frames.

"Just first-day nerves," I lie, wondering how much she knows about Gabriel's "arrangements" with his assistants.

"You'll do fine," she says with an unreadable smile. "Mr. Reed doesn't hire anyone who can't keep up."

She walks me through office protocols efficiently, the filing system, phone routing, client confidentiality. I take careful notes, trying to ignore the persistent throb between my legs whenever Gabriel moves within eyesight. Jackie explains she handles the general business operations while I'll be working directly with Gabriel on his specific matters and clients.

"I read your resume. You've graduated recently?" she asks.

"Last week," I confirm.

"And you interned at Jackson & Klein before?"

"For three months. It was a great experience." I don't bother mentioning what led me to leave. Not everyone needs to know my hardships after my mom got sick.

At 10:55, reception calls to announce that the Morrisons have arrived. Jackie gives me a reassuring pat before returning to her desk.

Gabriel emerges from his office looking imposing. "Ready?"

"Yes, sir—I mean, Mr. Reed," I correct quickly, touching my neck nervously.

His eyes darken momentarily as his gaze tracks my movement, but his expression stays neutral. "Follow my lead."

We head toward the conference room, his hand brushing my lower back. It's a touch that could seem merely guiding, but it sends electricity racing up my spine.

The conference room gleams with glass and chrome, overlooking the Hudson. There's a laptop set up for us and a pitcher of water and four glasses sitting in the middle of the table. A man in a suit examines a document at the table, looking up as we enter. Something in his expression makes my skin crawl.

"Gabriel," he says. "I see you've hired new…talent."

"Cameron," Gabriel acknowledges, his voice noticeably cooler. "This is Maya Williams, my new personal assistant. Maya, meet Cameron Webb, head of our corporate division."

The antagonism between them is obvious.

"Charmed," Cameron says, extending his hand.

I take it, and he holds on too long. His eyes move over me invasively rather than appreciatively. Unlike Gabriel's gaze, which makes me think filthy thoughts, Cameron's look makes me want to run.

"Gabriel always did have an eye for potential."

The way he emphasizes certain words gives his comment a sleazy undertone. I resist wiping my palm against my skirt to erase his touch.

"The Morrisons will be here momentarily," Gabriel says, dismissing Cameron without addressing him. "Maya, please distribute the portfolios."

I move to the stack on a credenza, bending carefully to get the portfolios off the bottom shelf. When I straighten, I catch Cameron watching where my skirt pulls across my ass. My skin crawls, and I'm suddenly hyperaware of my lack of underwear.

"I'll take those," Mr. Reed says, suddenly beside me. "Cameron, don't you have the Westfield deposition this morning?"

Cameron's smile doesn't reach his eyes. "Just wanted to welcome the newest addition to our little family." He nods to me. "We should have lunch today, Maya. I could share some insights about working here."

"Thank you, but my schedule is full with orientation," I say, matching his fake smile. I'd rather eat ramen in a bathroom stall than share a meal with him.

"Another time, then." He pauses at the door. "Oh, and Gabriel? The senior partners were asking about the Morrison deal. They're concerned about the regulatory hurdles."

Gabriel's jaw tightens. "The Morrison deal is proceeding exactly as planned."

After Cameron leaves, Gabriel turns to me. "Keep your distance from Cameron. He has a reputation for...complicating relationships within the firm."

"Noted," I say, straightening the portfolios. "I'll try to give him a wide berth."

Gabriel's eyes flash with something possessive that makes my stomach flutter. "Make sure you do. He's particularly interested in things I value."

My breath catches. Things he values? Does he value his personal assistants beyond what they do at work? The thought of Gabriel Reed actually caring for me makes my stomach flutter.

Before I can process his statement fully, the conference room door opens again and Jackie ushers in the Morrisons. Just like that, we're back to business, though my body remains aware of Gabriel's proximity.

CHAPTER 4

"This is my personal assistant, Maya Williams," Mr. Reed says to the Morrisons.

"Pleasure to meet you," I manage, hoping my voice sounds normal despite how turned on I am.

The Morrisons are a silver-haired couple in matching charcoal suits, and they give me polite smiles. The man's handshake is firm, while the woman studies me with the sharp assessment of someone who's spent decades in boardrooms.

"Maya will be taking notes today," Gabriel explains.

Mr. Reed holds my chair out for me, and as I slide into it, his hand brushes my shoulder. The touch looks professional to anyone watching, but it sends electric currents straight to my core. My brain conjures images of Mr. Reed bending me over this conference table, hiking up my skirt, and fucking me while everyone watches. A sudden surge of warmth courses through me at the thought.

The Morrisons settle in across the table from us, and I arrange my notepad and pen with shaking fingers. I click my pen repeatedly until I catch Mr. Reed's subtle glance. I immediately stop, embarrassed by my nervous habit. Focus, Maya. This is the biggest deal the firm has handled this year. I can't fuck this up just because I'm daydreaming about my boss doing unspeakably filthy things to me.

"As I was explaining on the phone," Mr. Morrison says, sliding documents across the polished table, "the restructuring timeline concerns us. We need guarantees about the international implications."

I stare at the legal documents, recognizing enough business terminology to follow along but feeling completely out of my depth. Two weeks ago, I was a struggling student serving coffee and cramming for finals. Now I'm sitting in high-level corporate meetings at a top law firm. Without panties. And lusting after the most gorgeous man I've ever seen in person—who's also my new boss. Seriously, what has my life become?

Gabriel responds to their concerns while I scribble notes. I catch him glancing at me. Does he know I'm already dripping wet? The way his jaw tightens slightly when our eyes meet tells me he does.

"Maya, could you pull up the subsidiary agreements?" Gabriel's tone is purely professional.

The what now? I have no idea where to find those files. I frantically tap at the laptop, hoping the panic isn't visible on my face. I'm going to look like a complete idiot on my first day.

"In the Morrison folder, under international holdings," Gabriel adds smoothly, saving me without drawing attention to my confusion.

While I'm accessing the folder, he reaches for his water glass and his hand brushes my arm. I'd assume it was an accident, except his fingers linger a fraction too long. A ripple of pleasure zips south and settles in my core.

"Here," I manage, pulling up the correct files while my skin burns where he touched me.

The Morrisons continue their discussion, unaware of the tension crackling between Gabriel and me. Tax implications, merger timelines, regulatory compliance—I should focus on absorbing everything I can. This is exactly the experience I hoped to get after college, but all I can think about is Gabriel's hands.

"The European markets pose the greatest challenge," Mrs. Morrison says. "Particularly the regulatory requirements in Germany."

I nod as if I understand while taking notes. Fake it until you make it, right? That's been my strategy since my mom died and I had to figure out how to survive on my own.

Gabriel moves his chair closer to mine, supposedly to review my notes. His thigh presses against mine under the table, and my legs quiver at the contact.

"Excellent summary," he murmurs, his breath warm against my ear as he leans over to read my screen. To everyone else, he's simply reviewing his assistant's work. To me, he's pure temptation in a tailored suit.

He rests his hand on my knee under the table, and it almost makes me jump in surprise. The table hides what he's doing underneath, and the warmth of his palm sends a ripple of pleasure up my thigh. I have to press my lips together to keep from moaning.

"Maya is new to our team," Gabriel says while tracing small circles against my knee with his thumb. His voice remains steady. "But she's already proving invaluable."

Is he serious? Praising me while touching me like this? I press my thighs together, trying to control the throbbing between my legs.

"Quick study?" Mr. Morrison asks.

Right now, my brain is so fried the only thing I'm studying is the way Gabriel's fingers feel against my skin. It takes considerable effort not to squirm in my seat.

"Extremely," Gabriel confirms.

His fingers graze the sensitive skin of my inner thigh, and I instinctively part my legs slightly while fighting to maintain my neutral expression. Jesus Christ, I'm such a slut for this man I barely know. I've never been this wet in my life.

Gabriel continues the business discussion while his hand creeps higher. "The timeline concerns are valid. We can address those through phased implementation."

My thighs quiver as his fingers inch closer to my pussy. The risk of being discovered should terrify me, but it's only making everything more intense. If the Morrisons knew what was happening under this table, they'd probably have heart attacks.

"Maya, do you have a background in international business?" Mrs. Morrison asks suddenly.

"I'm—" I clear my throat, struggling to form words. "I just graduated with a double major in business administration and legal studies."

Somehow my voice sounds steady, like I'm not seconds away from moaning in front of these important clients.

"That's wonderful," Mrs. Morrison says with an encouraging smile. "You're lucky to be working under Mr. Reed right out of college."

Heh, under Mr. Reed...it takes everything in my power not to snicker.

"She's going to get valuable hands-on experience," Gabriel agrees, and his fingers brush against my pussy.

My body buzzes from his touch, and for a terrifying second, I think I might actually orgasm. Holy fuck, I'm going to come in front of clients on my first day. I'll be fired before lunch.

Before I come, he pulls his hand away. He returns to his professional behavior while I sit there trembling and my face burning with arousal.

"I think we have everything we need for the preliminary assessment," Gabriel announces and stands. "Maya will organize our notes, and Jackie will prepare the timeline for your review."

The Morrisons gather their materials, shaking hands and discussing follow-up meetings. Normal business interactions while I stand there on unsteady legs.

"Welcome to Reed & Associates," Mrs. Morrison says to me with a smile, and I manage to thank her without making a fool of myself.

The moment the conference room door closes behind them, Gabriel turns to me.

"Your notes," he says simply.

I hand him my notepad, watching his eyes scan my chaotic scribbles. Despite everything that just happened, I captured the key points. My normal note-taking system was completely abandoned in favor of just getting the information down while being sexually tortured.

"Not bad for your first client meeting. You'll improve quickly," he says, closing the notepad. "Now for other business. Come to my office."

His voice leaves no room for argument. Excitement surges through my veins in response to his command. I follow him through the glass doors, my legs still unsteady. The moment we're inside his office, he closes the door and turns on the privacy screen.

He stands directly in front of me. "How do you feel?"

"Like I'm going to combust," I admit, breathless. "My pussy is—"

He interrupts me. "I know exactly how your pussy is. I felt it."

Lust rushes through me at his words. Yeah, I guess he does.

He reaches into his pocket and pulls out my panties. He holds them out to me. "You earned these back."

I take them with shaking hands. "Thank you."

"Put them on," he commands softly.

My body throbs at his tone. I step out of my heels and slide the fabric up my legs. The moisture immediately soaks the cotton.

"Better?" Gabriel asks, watching me with those intense eyes.

"Not really. Now I'm just wet and covered."

He laughs, and my chest lightens with unexpected joy. "We'll address that after hours. Right now, we have work to do."

Just like that, we're back to business. I'm learning this is how he operates. Complete control of the situation, the timing, my responses.

"What do I need to do now?" I ask, trying to regain my composure while my panties stick uncomfortably to my skin.

"Jackie will handle the Morrison timeline," he says, moving to his desk, every inch the commanding attorney again. "You need to familiarize yourself with how things run around here. Think you can work?"

"Yes, sir."

His eyes flash with approval and something darker, more promising. "Good girl."

Those two words send heat racing through me all over again. I'm getting off on praise from my boss after nearly orgasming in front of clients. And I'm not even a little sorry about it.

As I settle at my desk to read through the orientation materials, I'm hyperaware of Gabriel watching me through the glass partition. Of the dampness between my legs. Of the promise in his voice when he said "after hours."

My fingers hover over the keyboard as I try to concentrate on the words on my screen instead of the throbbing between my legs. But my mind keeps returning to how Mr. Reed's fingers felt brushing against my pussy.

I glance through the glass to find him watching me still, his expression unreadable but intense.

Oh yeah, my new boss could ruin me in the best possible way.

CHAPTER 5

After lunch, Gabriel summons me to his office. I grab a notepad and pen. I am a professional, after all.

The privacy screen hums to life as he closes the door behind us, making my heart rate speed up.

"Sit," Gabriel commands, gesturing to the chair across from his desk.

I perch on the edge and track his movements as he circles behind the desk with predatory calm.

"Your performance in that meeting was exceptional," he says, voice laced with that authoritative edge that makes my pussy ache.

"Thank you," I manage, though the words come out breathy. I click my pen, desperate for something to do with my hands.

"However..." He shrugs off his suit jacket and drapes it neatly over the back of his chair. "There's still room for improvement."

What? I documented everything and held it together while he was caressing me. What could I have possibly messed up on?

"Your focus wavered," he continues, rolling up his sleeves. "Understandable, given the circumstances. But it's unacceptable going forward."

Is he kidding? He was the one fingering me under the conference table! I should protest, but one glance at his muscular forearms makes my brain go fuzzy.

"I maintained complete professionalism," I insist, finding my backbone while my fingers twist the sleeve of my blouse nervously.

"Did you?" He steps around the desk and stops directly in front of me. "Then tell me: what was Morrison's primary concern about the European subsidiary structure?"

Fuck. My mind blanks. I click the pen more rapidly. "The...regulatory timeline?"

"Incorrect." His tone stays even, but something dangerous flickers in his eyes. "Their primary concern was liability distribution across jurisdictions. The timeline was secondary."

Embarrassment floods my cheeks. He's right. I was so busy fighting back moans while he touched me I missed the bigger point.

"I see you understand," Gabriel says, reading my expression. "Which brings us to your performance evaluation."

"My what?" This is day one. I'm obviously not getting a real performance evaluation, but heat coils through me at the idea of being disciplined. I've never been spanked, but my body's reaction to him suggests I might enjoy it.

"Stand up."

I rise on shaky legs. Gabriel moves behind me, and I shift from foot to foot, struggling for composure.

"Before we continue," he murmurs, his warm breath brushing my ear, "I need your explicit consent. Tell me your boundaries."

His question throws me. I didn't expect consideration from a man who commands every molecule in the room.

My voice cracks. "I don't want to be really hurt. And I need to know this won't affect my actual job review. The real one."

Mr. Reed rests his hand on my shoulder. "Your advancement depends solely on merit. Always. And I would never cause you genuine pain unless you ask for it." His voice lowers. "Now say your safe words."

"Red to stop. Yellow to slow down. Green to continue," I recite, recalling the contract.

"Use them without hesitation if needed." His tone snaps back to iron authority, making my pussy clench. "Now, hands on the desk."

My heart slams against my ribs like a caged animal. This is straight out of those spicy novels I devour whenever I have free time, except this is real.

"Gabriel," I moan.

"Sir," he corrects. "When we're alone, you call me sir."

My pussy flutters at his tone. "Sir, what're you doing?"

"Teaching you the importance of paying attention."

He presses on my shoulder, guiding me forward until my palms flatten against the cool mahogany.

Jesus Christ. This is happening. Right here. In his office. In the middle of the damn day.

I lean forward, raising my ass obediently, every inch of me tingling from being exposed and aroused.

"Good girl." He drags his hands down my back, tracing my spine through the silk of my blouse. "Now, let's talk about your attention to detail."

He raises the hem of my skirt slowly, and cool air brushes my thighs. I resist the urge to push back against him while my body flares with anticipation.

"These wet panties," he says, hooking a finger under the waistband, "prove how distracted you've been."

The cotton sticks to my soaked, swollen flesh. He's right.

"They have to go." He peels the damp fabric down my legs. I step out of them carefully, leaving them pooled on his office floor. The air conditioning kicks in, and the rush of air against my bare skin sends a shiver up my spine.

He plants his palm on my bare ass. "Now you'll learn what happens when my assistant loses focus during important meetings."

Suddenly, the intercom crackles to life.

I freeze, muscles locking tight. Gabriel doesn't lift his hand from my butt. Oh God, oh God, oh God. What if someone realizes what we're doing?

"Gabriel?" Cameron Webb's voice slithers through the speaker. "We need to discuss the Morrison regulatory issues. Jackie said you were busy, but this can't wait."

Cameron. The man whose gaze made my skin crawl earlier.

Gabriel's fingers bite into my hip. It's the first flicker of real tension I've ever seen in him. He leans forward, caging me against the desk as he smashes the intercom button.

"Not now, Cameron," he growls. "I'll find you when I'm finished."

"The senior partners are asking questions. Give me five minutes," Cameron insists.

I look back at Gabriel, and his jaw flexes. "One hour, Cameron. Not a minute sooner."

There's a brief pause before Cameron responds with a snarl. "Fine. But they won't be happy about the delay."

When the intercom shuts off, Mr. Reed exhales. The tension loosens in his shoulders. "Cameron doesn't respect boundaries," he mutters, hitting the Do Not Disturb button on his phone. "Never has. My father thought that made him the perfect attorney."

This is the first personal share about his past. There's unspoken pain there.

He snaps back into his commanding tone. "That is why focus matters. One careless moment could have exposed us both."

He's right. If I'd made a sound or let anything slip, my career at the firm would be dead before it even started. I can't lose this job. I literally can't afford to.

"Do you understand?" He slips his hand between my thighs and rubs my pussy.

I do my best to hold back a moan. "Yes, sir."

He circles my clit with excruciating lightness, teasing me. The gentle strokes sizzle my brain. I rock back, desperate for more, but he pulls away immediately.

"Patience," he warns. "You need to learn control."

My legs tremble as he continues the relentless torture. His touch ignites every nerve without granting release. My pussy clenches helplessly, hungry and empty. I grip the desk, trying not to moan.

"Please," I whisper.

"Please what?" His tone slices through me, calm as ever.

"Please, sir. I need—" I break off as I shiver from pleasure.

"What do you need, Maya?"

"I need more," I choke out.

"More what?" His finger presses at my entrance, applying just enough pressure to drive me insane. "Be specific."

"Please, sir. I need you to fuck me," I moan out, past shame and pride.

"There's my honest girl." He sinks one finger inside me, making me bite down a cry.

He adds a second finger, stretching me open while his thumb returns to my clit. The dual sensation short-circuits my brain. My back bows as bliss explodes in my core, blooming through every inch of me.

He finger-fucks me slowly. "This is what happens when you please me."

I clench around him, drunk on his praise, dizzy from the power in his words.

He pulls his fingers free. "And this is what happens when you disappoint me."

"Nooooo," I whimper, rocking my hips shamelessly in search of his hand. "Please don't stop."

"Then convince me you've learned your lesson."

I pant, "I have. I'll do better. I'll stay focused. I swear." If I don't get his cock inside me, I'm going to go insane.

"Prove it."

The sounds of his belt buckle being undone and the hiss of his zipper makes my head spin.

"Tell me about Morrison's liability concerns," he orders as he presses the tip of his cock against my pussy.

What the hell? He wants me to discuss corporate law while he's fucking me? this is like Suits, except ten times filthier and definitely not safe for cable TV.

"I can't think when you're—" I stammer, my words breaking apart.

"Then learn to multitask." He pushes in slowly. "Liability distribution. Explain it."

He pauses halfway inside, holding still, waiting.

I gasp, "The...the European subsidiaries create potential exposure across multiple jurisdictions."

"Good." He pulls out and then sinks into me again. "Keep going."

My mind fractures under the rhythm. It's slow, punishing strokes that scatter my thoughts like confetti.

"Morrison wants protection from—" I moan as he hits a pleasurable spot deep inside me. "From cross-border litigation."

His pace quickens just enough to push me closer to the edge. "Excellent. And our proposed solution?"

I'm bent over my boss's desk, getting fucked senseless while he's grilling me about work. And somehow, it's the hottest, filthiest thing I've ever experienced. Each thrust lights me up.

"Structured—oh God—structured liability caps with jurisdiction-specific clauses," I choke out, biting my lip to hold back a scream.

"Perfect." His hand snakes around to my clit, circling it. "You think clearly with the right motivation."

The combination of his cock inside me and his fingers on my clit builds a molten pressure in my belly. My legs tremble, threatening to collapse.

"Sir," I gasp. "I'm going to come."

"Not yet." His movements slow to an agonizing grind. "Not until I say."

I whimper as I feel every nerve in my body stretched to its limit. He keeps up the torment, dragging me to the edge again and again without letting me fall.

"Please," I beg, clinging to the desk and trying to press backwards to get him to fuck me harder. "Please let me come."

"Why should I?" His voice is gruff with need, but his control never wavers.

"Because I learned my lesson. Because I'll never lose focus again. Because"—my voice splinters, desperate—"because this job means everything to me and I can't afford to fail and you're the most incredible man I've ever met and—"

"Because you're mine," he cuts in, driving harder, as if staking a claim. "Because you belong to me in this office and everywhere else. And because I'm going to breed this tight pussy of yours until you're so full of my cum you can't think."

Uh, breed? I'm not on birth control. He really could breed me. The filthiness drives me wild, and suddenly, I want the risk.

"Yes," I sob, frantic. "I'm yours. Breed me!"

He presses down on my clit. "Now come for me like the good girl you are."

My body detonates as pleasure rips through me in blinding waves. I slap a hand over my mouth to muffle my cries as my body clenches around him. I tremble, completely undone.

"Fuck, time for your first breeding," Gabriel groans, losing his last shred of control as my pussy milks him. He thrusts deep one last time as spurts of warm cum bathe my inner walls. Feeling his cum triggers another smaller orgasm from me that leaves me shaking.

He keeps his cock buried inside me while we catch our breaths. Once we both come down, he slowly withdraws before helping me stand.

My legs threaten to buckle, but he catches me against his chest, anchoring me. I smooth my blouse with trembling hands, trying to find a scrap of composure.

"You did well," he murmurs into my hair.

His tenderness surprises me, and I lean against him, still reeling. "That was..."

"Necessary," he finishes. "You needed to understand the stakes. The importance of control, no matter the circumstances."

I don't bother to tell him if he wasn't messing with me, I wouldn't need control. The orgasm was too good for me to complain about his methods.

"I understand," I say softly.

Gabriel retrieves my panties from the floor, handing them to me, and watches while I slip them back on. The cotton instantly clings, already damp from earlier, plus now his cum is dripping out of me.

"Clean yourself up," he orders, sliding back into his crisp professional mask as he straightens his clothes. "I need to handle Cameron. Meet me in the law library at five. We have research to finish for the Morrison timeline."

The law library?

"Yes, sir," I breathe, heading for his private bathroom.

"Maya."

I freeze at the doorway and look back at him.

"Next time you lose focus in a meeting," he warns, smoothing down his tie, "the consequences will be more severe."

My body tingles at the promise in his voice. More severe? Is this supposed to scare me? He just rocked my world and talked about breeding me, and now he's promising me more if I misbehave. What's the incentive to behave?

"Understood," I manage, biting my lip to keep from grinning like an unhinged groupie.

Inside his bathroom, I study myself in the mirror: flushed cheeks, tousled hair, eyes glittering with satisfaction. I look like a woman who was just thoroughly fucked by her boss.

And it's only the first day of work.

CHAPTER 6

The law library instantly impresses me with its floor-to-ceiling bookshelves, polished mahogany tables, and that rich, unmistakable scent of old books mixed with furniture wax.

I spot Gabriel at a table with two open laptops. He glances up as I approach, and his expression is all business except for that simmering desire in his eyes when they lock on mine.

"The Morrison regulatory precedents," he says, gesturing to his screen. "We need to establish a solid ground for our jurisdictional approach."

I sink into the chair beside him, hyper-aware of the dampness between my thighs. Even after cleaning up, I've stayed wet all afternoon thinking about him railing me over his desk.

"Concentrate," he murmurs, catching my wandering mind. "Anyone could walk in at any moment."

He's right. The library is quiet for now, but other attorneys cycle through constantly.

"I'm trying," I say, my voice steadier than I feel.

Gabriel slides the second laptop toward me and helps me log into the research database. He doesn't need to show me what to do since I used the database in college.

We settle into a rhythm. The only sounds are our breathing and the occasional mouse click. Gradually, the legal complexities pull me in, giving my arousal a chance to simmer beneath the surface while my mind engages the challenge.

"You grasp this material better than most first-year associates," Gabriel observes after I flag a precedent buried in a complex regulatory ruling.

"I've done well in my business law classes," I admit, a tingle of pride warming me. "It's not Harvard, but..."

"Results matter more than where you got your diploma," he says when I don't finish my thought. "At least to a point. Though my father believed results were everything. That's why Cameron became his protégé. He admired Cameron's...flexible ethics."

A shadow crosses Gabriel's face. There it is again, a hint of a complicated family history.

"Your father was a lawyer too?" I ask carefully.

Gabriel meets my gaze, and for a brief second, I catch a flicker of vulnerability behind all that steel. "He was a senior partner at Reed & Associates before I removed him. Once I had significant ownership, I restructured the firm and brought in new senior partners."

Holy shit. I should have done better research about the firm. Gabriel took over his father's empire and reshaped it.

Before I can push for details, footsteps echo down the hall. Gabriel's features shift instantly back to professional. A security guard rounds the corner, nodding politely.

"Just on my rounds, Mr. Reed," the guard says. "I didn't realize anyone was in here."

"We're just finishing research," Gabriel replies smoothly. Beneath the table, his hand settles on my knee, hidden from sight. "We'll be done shortly."

The guard nods and continues on his route. Gabriel's fingers trace slow, teasing circles on my knee, the motion casual on the surface but sparking a jolt of lust that travels up my thigh, as it reminds me of the conference room earlier.

"I believe we need to get back to establishing sufficient precedent," he says, voice calm and measured while his fingers creep higher.

I open my legs to give him better access, and my clit throbs. Again?

"Yes, sir," I manage, my voice cracking as his fingertips brush the seam of damp cotton. I read over case files while his touch makes my pussy throb, and I whisper, "The regulatory framework supports our position."

"Does it?" His finger brushes over my pussy. "Explain the jurisdictional precedent."

This is torture. Sweet, perfect torture. "The Third Circuit ruling in Johnson v. International Holdings establishes that—" I moan as he presses against my clit through the cotton. "Cross-border liability requires explicit contractual frameworks."

"Good girl." His approval sends heat racing through me. "Keep going."

I pretend to read while he slides his hand higher. The risk makes every-thing more intense. Anyone could walk in–another attorney working late, security making rounds again, or the cleaning staff.

"The European Union regulations create additional compliance re-quirements," I continue, my voice steady despite the way his fingers tease me. "Particularly regarding data protection and—oh God—and subsidiary reporting structures."

His finger slips beneath my panties, and I fight the urge to moan.

"You're soaked," he murmurs. "My good little assistant, getting wet while discussing corporate law."

"Sir," I breathe, opening my legs even wider.

"Tell me about the German regulatory framework," he commands, slid-ing one finger inside me while his palm grinds against my clit.

My head spins. I'm getting fingered in the law library at my new job. "The German Corporate Governance Code requires—fuck—requires en-hanced disclosure for foreign subsidiaries."

He adds a second finger. "Excellent, and the compliance timeline?"

I grip the side of the table, trying to stay quiet as he finger-fucks me. "Eighteen months for full implementation, with quarterly reporting." I break off as he massages that perfect spot inside me.

"Finish your thought."

"Quarterly reporting to regulatory authorities," I gasp.

"Hmm, your pussy is so ready to be filled. So eager to take my seed. I bet you'd let me breed you right here in the library, wouldn't you?"

The thought of him coming inside me here, of his cum filling me where anyone could walk in, makes my pussy clench around his fingers.

Footsteps echo in the hallway again, and Gabriel freezes with his fingers still in my pussy. We both hold still and listen as a security guard passes by our section.

The footsteps fade, and Gabriel resumes his torment.

"Such a good sub," he whispers. "Learning to focus despite distractions."

My thighs tremble as he brings me closer to the edge. "Please," I whisper, desperate.

"Please what?"

"Please let me come, sir."

"Not yet." He slows his movements to an agonizing pace. "First, tell me why you think Cameron is questioning our approach."

What? I can barely think with his fingers inside me, and he wants me to analyze office politics on my first day of the job?

"He thinks..." It's almost impossible to form coherent thoughts. "He thinks you're taking unnecessary risks with the regulatory timeline."

"And what do you think?"

His thumb presses against my clit, making my back arch. "It seems like he's trying to undermine you. Make the senior partners doubt your judgment."

"Smart girl." Gabriel's fingers curl inside me, finding that spot that makes me see stars. "And what should we do about it?"

I pant, "Document everything. Create a paper trail. Make it impossible for him to claim incompetence if anything goes wrong."

"Perfect." His pace increases, driving me toward the edge. "You understand the game now."

"Yes, sir." My voice cracks as the pressure builds in my core.

"You've earned your reward. You can come."

His fingers speed up, and my orgasm crashes through me. I press my lips together to keep from crying out as waves of pleasure roll through me. Gabriel finger-fucks me slowly as I ride out the aftershocks, and I'm shaking and breathless when he removes his hand.

He brings his fingers to his mouth, tasting me while maintaining eye contact. "Delicious," he murmurs, making my face burn with arousal and embarrassment.

I adjust my skirt and panties with trembling hands. "Mr. Reed..."

"Sir," he corrects automatically.

"Sir, what happens now?"

His eyes darken. "Now you go home and think about how easily you lost control. How much you loved it."

He's right. I'm already addicted to him and the way he makes me feel.

He closes his laptop. "Tomorrow, you continue learning what it means to be mine."

Mine. The word sends a pulse of pleasure through me. "Yes, sir."

He stands and helps me to my feet. If anyone was watching us, I don't think they'd know he just made me orgasm.

"Your performance today was exceptional," he says as we walk toward his private elevator by his office. "Both professionally and personally."

An unexpected surge of pride simmers in my chest. "Thank you, sir."

The elevator arrives, and we step inside. The moment the doors close, Gabriel slams his hand against the emergency stop button. Immediately, the car jolts to a halt. Before I can process what's happening, he has me pinned against the wall.

"What are you—"

His mouth crashes onto mine, swallowing my words. This isn't the controlled Gabriel from the library. This is something raw, unleashed. His tongue pushes past my lips as his hands grip my ass, lifting me against him.

"Wrap your legs around me," he growls against my mouth.

My body responds before my brain can catch up. I hook my ankles behind his back as he grinds his hard cock against my pussy.

"The cameras!" I gasp.

"Disabled just for today," he says, his teeth grazing my neck.

Holy fuck, he planned this? I cling to his shoulders as he reaches between us, unfastening his pants with one hand while the other supports my weight. My heart hammers so hard I think it might burst through my chest.

"I need to be inside you. Now."

He shoves my panties aside, and in one swift thrust, he fills me. I cry out, not caring if anyone hears us through the elevator doors. He fucks me hard against the wall, each thrust lifting me higher.

"Look at me," he demands.

His eyes burn into mine when I look at him, all pretense of control shattered. This isn't my boss or even my dom. This is just Gabriel, desperate and wanting.

"I haven't been able to think about anything but breeding you all day," he confesses, his voice ragged.

"Me too," I whimper as he hits that perfect spot inside me. "Oh God, me too."

His pace becomes frantic, almost brutal. I'm going to have bruises tomorrow from where the elevator rail digs into my back, and I don't care. I want them. Want the reminder.

"Come for me," he commands. "One more time."

My orgasm hits like a freight train, more intense than the one in the library. I convulse around him, nails digging into his shoulders through his expensive suit. He follows immediately, burying his face in my neck to muffle his groan as he unloads ropes of warm cum inside me.

For three heartbeats, we stay frozen and breathless, stunned by our own recklessness.

Then Gabriel reaches out and releases the emergency stop. The elevator hums back to life as he carefully sets me down, both of us frantically adjusting our clothes.

By the time the doors open to the parking garage, we look presentable again, except for my flushed cheeks and his slightly loosened tie.

"My driver will take you home," Gabriel says, his voice back to its usual controlled tone, though I can hear the slight breathlessness beneath it.

The driver is waiting with the black Audi. Gabriel helps me into the backseat, his hand lingering on mine just a moment longer than necessary.

"Good night, Maya."

"Good night, Mr. Reed," I reply, playing my part while my lips still tingle from his kiss and my body hums with satisfaction.

As the car glides through Manhattan traffic, my phone pings with a text message.

Mr. Reed:

> Sleep well. Tomorrow we begin the real work.

I stare at the message, my pussy still throbbing from the wild fucking in the elevator. The real work? What the hell have we been doing so far?

Another ping from my phone.

Mr. Reed:

> And Maya? Wear the black skirt again tomorrow.
> Your legs look fabulous in it.

My face burns as I type back.

Mr. Reed:

Good girl.

As the car pulls up to my building, I realize I'm in deeper than I ever imagined. This isn't just about a job anymore or even just about incredible sex.

This is about belonging to Gabriel Reed, and a small part of me hopes I get pregnant, despite knowing the timing is bad.

I want it more than I've ever wanted anything in my life.

Even if I'm terrified of what that means.

Chapter 7

The next evening, I stretch in Gabriel's leather chair, my neck aching from hunching over the Morrison deal for three hours. The rest of the building is quiet since everyone else left, but I wanted to finish the international compliance section before tomorrow's meeting.

It's been a long day of Gabriel driving me crazy with brief touches, but it's also been a busy day, and he had to leave earlier for dinner with a client. I know we can't have sex in the office all the time, but I was hoping for something more today.

I brought my laptop into his office, and it feels a little naughty to be working in here. He never said I couldn't, but he also never said I could...

The chair swivels as I lean back. His chair. The one he sits in when he's commanding his empire and making million-dollar decisions.

I daydream about yesterday when he bent me over his desk, and a bolt of desire shoots straight to my core at the memory. Focus, Maya. Work first, fantasies later.

I turn back to my laptop, but the words blur. It's past nine, and my brain is mush. Through the floor-to-ceiling windows, the Financial District glitters below. Maybe just a five-minute break in his ridiculously comfortable chair won't hurt. I close my eyes, letting myself sink into the buttery leather. The faint scent of his cologne lingers and relaxes me.

The elevator dings.

My eyes snap open. Shit. Hopefully, it's just security making rounds. I scramble to get out of Gabriel's chair, but the sound of confident footsteps freezes me in place.

If it's Gabriel, what am I supposed to say? Sorry, just pretending to be important in your incredibly expensive chair while fantasizing about yesterday's desk activities?

Gabriel appears in his office doorway. He's still in his suit, but he's loosened his tie. His eyes immediately zero in on me in his chair. "Well, this is interesting."

"I was just...the timeline needed...I can explain. This isn't what it looks like, except it's exactly what it looks like, which is me being completely inappropriate and—"

He steps into his office, closing the door. "My assistant, in my chair, after hours."

I can't read his expression, which terrifies and excites me. Is he angry? Amused?

"I'm sorry," I start to rise, adjusting my blouse nervously. "I shouldn't be here. I was just tired, and it looked so comfortable, and I figured what's the harm in sitting for like two seconds, but then it felt really nice and—"

"Stay."

The command stops me mid-motion and mid-ramble. I sit back down.

He approaches the desk, and I try not to squirm. I'm such a slut that I'm getting turned on by being caught red-handed.

He stands beside me. "Tell me, what does it feel like?"

"What does what feel like?" I fidget with my pen, clicking it nervously.

"Sitting in my chair. Behind my desk." He brushes his fingers along my shoulder. "Having that view from my office."

"Powerful," I admit. "And like I'm pretending to be someone I'm not."

His fingers trace along my shoulder blade through my silk blouse. "Exactly. Power is intoxicating. Addictive."

"I wasn't trying to—" I start, then stop. Who am I kidding? "Okay, maybe I liked the feeling of power. Just a little. It's like being the heroine in one of those billionaire romance novels, except instead of seducing the CEO, I'm just trying not to mess up your very expensive office furniture."

His smile transforms his face from stern to playful. "There's my honest girl."

He straightens, moving to the window that overlooks the city. "Do you know what I see when I sit in that chair?"

"No, what?"

"Every case I've won, every client I've gained, every decision that brought me here." He turns back to me. "And now, when I sit there, I'll see you."

My pulse quickens at the possessiveness in his voice. "Gabriel,,,"

"Sir," he corrects.

"Sir," I breathe, biting my lip. "What're you doing here so late? I thought you had dinner with the client from Boston."

"I have a conference call with Tokyo. Deal negotiations that couldn't wait." He checks his watch. "Which starts in ten minutes."

The implication hangs between us. He has work to do, and I'm sitting in his chair like some kind of distraction. I cross and uncross my legs, suddenly aware of how inappropriate this whole situation is.

"I should go," I say, starting to rise again. "I'll just grab my stuff."

"Should you?" His voice stops me.

What does that mean? I search his face for clues, finding only that intensity that makes my skin prickle. I click my pen more quickly, nervous energy coursing through me.

"The call will last thirty minutes," he continues. "Important clients. A significant deal involving cross-border acquisition structures."

I nod, not sure where this is going but fascinated despite myself.

"I'll need to focus entirely on the negotiation." His eyes meet mine. "Despite any...distractions."

Oh. Oh fuck. Is he suggesting that I do something while he's on the call?

"What kind of distractions?" I ask, my voice embarrassingly breathy.

Instead of answering, he reaches for his belt buckle and my mouth goes dry.

"The kind that tests a man's control," he says, moving to his zipper. "The kind that requires absolute silence."

Jesus Christ. My pulse hammers so hard I'm sure he can hear it. "Sir, are you asking me to—because if you are, that's like something out of a really inappropriate office fantasy, which I definitely don't have, except apparently I do now, and—" I cut myself off, not wanting to sound nervous.

He smiles. "Before we continue, are you comfortable with what I'm suggesting?"

The question catches me off guard. Even in the middle of what's clearly turning into another hot-as-hell encounter, he's checking my boundaries.

My words come out in a rush. "Yes. Green. Completely green."

"Good." He nods, satisfied. "I'm not asking anything," he continues as he pulls his cock out of his pants and boxers. "I'm simply conducting business while my assistant remains close by."

My eyes drop to his cock. It's thick and absolutely gorgeous. I've felt him inside me, but this is the first time I'm really seeing him. All of him. Holy fuck.

"Get under the desk," he commands softly.

Yep, this is happening. I'm about to crawl under my boss's desk to suck his cock during a meeting. And I've never wanted anything more.

I slide from the chair to my knees, the plush carpet soft as I crawl into the space beneath his massive desk. Gabriel settles into his chair, his legs blocking me in.

"Comfortable?" he asks, his voice taking on that edge of command.

"Yes." Thank God I'm not claustrophobic.

From this position, I'm eye-level with his cock, close enough to see the bead of moisture at the tip and to smell his arousal mixed with expensive soap. I adjust my position, trying to find the best angle to approach this.

His phone buzzes. He answers it with, "Gabriel Reed speaking."

Multiple voices from the conference call fill the office, and Gabriel responds with his usual composure. I move between his thighs and hover my head over his cock. He moves a hand under the desk and tangles it in my hair, applying gentle pressure that's unmistakable. A command.

I lean forward, pressing a soft kiss to the head and smile as his cock jerks. Gabriel's voice never wavers as he discusses market projections, but his fingers tighten in my hair.

"The due diligence timeline must accommodate both SEC requirements and international disclosure standards," Gabriel continues while I part my lips and sink down on his cock.

This is crazy. The risk of being discovered makes everything more erotic. I've had boyfriends who liked to be in charge before, but it was never like this.

I work my tongue around his length, savoring the saltiness of him. His sharp intake of breath is barely noticeable, covered by his response to a client question about subsidiary structures.

I establish a steady rhythm, taking him deeper, hollowing my cheeks as I work. Gabriel's other hand grips the arm of his chair, knuckles white with the effort of maintaining control. He continues the business discussion, but I catch a slight roughness creeping into his voice.

Suddenly, footsteps sound in the hallway outside. I freeze with Gabriel's cock still in my mouth as the footsteps slow near his office door.

"Just a moment; I'm receiving some documents," Gabriel says into the phone, his voice controlled despite the tension I can feel in his thighs.

There's a knock at the door, and I feel faint.

"Gabriel?" Cameron Webb opens the door. "Security said you were still here. We have things to discuss."

Fuck, fuck, fuck. The back of the desk goes all the way to the floor, so I know he can't see me, but the fear of discovery still lights me up with twisted arousal. I remain absolutely still, Gabriel's cock pulsing against my tongue as he responds.

"I'm on a call with Tokyo, Cameron," he says, his voice betraying none of the tension radiating from him. "Whatever it is, can wait until tomorrow. Nine a.m., my office."

"Fine, but you'd better be willing to talk tomorrow. By the way, where's your new assistant? Security mentioned she was working late too."

My blood runs cold. Is Cameron checking up on me?

"Maya already left," Gabriel lies smoothly. "Is there anything else? My Tokyo clients are waiting."

"No, nothing else." Another pause. "For now."

The door closes, and Gabriel lets out a long breath before returning to his call.

"My apologies for the interruption," he says. "As I was saying, the cross-border transfer pricing agreements..."

I'm still electrified from the near-discovery, and I resume my attention to Gabriel's cock, working him more enthusiastically than before. The contradiction is intoxicating. This powerful man commanding deals while I worship him with my mouth, both of us nearly caught by Cameron.

"—finalize the subsidiary documentation and cross-border transfer pricing agreements by Friday," Gabriel concludes, his voice tight.

I redouble my efforts, taking him as deep as I can while my hand works the base of his cock. His fingers tighten in my hair, a silent warning that he's about to lose control. I double down, wanting to make him come.

"I'll have my team prepare the documentation package," Gabriel says, and his cock pulses a second before he explodes.

He barely makes a sound, just a sharp exhale that could be mistaken for frustration. I swallow his cum as quickly as I can, determined not to lose a drop. I keep sucking and licking on him to clean him up.

"Excellent. I'll coordinate with our international counsel and speak with you tomorrow," Gabriel says, ending the call.

The moment he hangs up, his careful control cracks. "Fuck, Maya."

I release his cock slowly, pressing one last kiss to the tip before sitting on my heels. Gabriel pushes his chair back so he can see me. His eyes glitter with satisfaction and something deeper. Is that affection?

"Come here," he says softly.

I climb out from under his desk, and he pulls me onto his lap, cradling me against his chest.

"You were incredible," he murmurs against my hair. "Absolutely incredible."

My chest tightens with happiness, and I giggle at him. "That was like watching a masterclass in self-control. Is that a natural Gabriel Reed superpower?"

"Years of practice." He strokes my back. "My father believed that showing emotion was weakness. He always had to be in control no matter where he was at; the courtroom, boardroom, or at home."

I like it when he tells me tiny details about his personal life. I stay quiet, afraid of breaking the spell.

Gabriel continues, his voice hardening. "Cameron learned my father's lessons well. Including how to exploit others' vulnerabilities."

"I don't like him," I whisper.

Gabriel's nostrils flare briefly. "Cameron doesn't just bend rules, he breaks them. When I discovered he was pressuring junior associates into sexual relationships in exchange for case assignments, I confronted my father."

"What happened?"

"My father said I was too soft. That power came with privileges. That's when I realized I didn't want his legacy. I wanted something better."

"So you took it from him. And remade it."

"I bought out his partners, removed him, and restructured the entire operation. My father was running this place into the ground, and it took a lot of work to get back to the top." Gabriel's voice turns bitter.

"Cameron remained because the senior partners protected him. Which is why Cameron hates me. I took what he thought would be his when my father retired. Now he goes after things he knows I want."

The weight of this revelation makes me blink, and the pieces click into place. This isn't just office politics.

"That's why he's watching me. He thinks I'm your weakness."

"Yes." Gabriel's arms tighten around me, and he suddenly changes the topic. "Have dinner with me this weekend. Outside the office."

His tone of voice makes it sound like he's asking for a date, and my heart skips a beat. Being seen together publicly is a big deal. Does he want more than just a physical relationship?

"I'd like that," I say softly.

His smile transforms his face. "Good. Because I have plans for us. Plans that extend far beyond this office."

As he helps me stand, I catch my reflection in the dark window. My hair is a mess, and I'm flushed. I look like a woman who just sucked her boss's cock under his desk. My body hums with pleasure. I really am such a slut. It's glorious.

"It's late. You need sleep," Gabriel says, returning to his professional demeanor as he straightens his clothes.

"Yes, Gabriel," I respond automatically as I start to leave. I'm still so turned on that sleep might be difficult.

His name rolls through my mind again—Gabriel, not Mr. Reed, or sir—and the intimacy of it still thrills me. In the office, surrounded by others, I carefully maintain the professional distance of *Mr. Reed,* but alone like this, I can get away with just Gabriel. My Gabriel. The way he looked at me tonight, with that flash of vulnerability when he mentioned his father, makes the name feel like a secret password to parts of him no one else gets to see.

"Maya."

His voice stops me at the door, and I look back.

"Next time you want to sit in my chair, ask permission first," he says, straightening his tie. "But don't stop wanting it," he adds, his eyes holding mine. "Ambition looks good on you."

My face burns with embarrassment and arousal. "I'll remember."

As I leave his office, I touch my lips. They're still swollen from the blowjob, and I know Gabriel is starting to claim more than just my body.

I gather my things and head for the elevator, and suddenly realize something fundamental has shifted between us. This isn't just about him being in control anymore. This is about teaching me to want control too. To want his world.

And hell yes, I'm ready to learn. Even if I'm terrified of how much I want it.

As the elevator descends toward the lobby, my phone pings with a text. I expect Gabriel, but the message isn't from a contact in my phone.

Unknown number:

> Enjoying your late nights with Gabriel? But be careful. He discards his toys when he's finished playing with them – C.

My blood runs cold. Cameron.

I stare at the glowing screen as the elevator reaches the lobby. Gabriel's warning about Cameron trying to take what's his suddenly feels more real. The game just got more dangerous.

Chapter 8

It's been a month of working with Gabriel, and it's been a blur of professional triumphs, stolen moments in the office, and intimate dinners on the weekend. I've learned more about corporate law and my own desires than I thought possible.

But something's changed. I catch myself watching him when he's working, admiring more than just his body or the way he commands a room. I notice how he remembers the cleaning staff's names, how his eyes soften when he talks about his cases helping real people.

Tonight, he's taking me out to dinner with clients. I smooth my black dress as Gabriel's driver pulls up to The Ivory Room. The dress cost me more than I used to make in two shifts at the diner, but it's worth it. It's simple, sophisticated, and hopefully impressive enough for whatever Gabriel has planned.

Gabriel's palm settles on my knee. "Nervous?"

My pulse jumps at his touch. Four weeks of working together, of him dominating me in his office, the law library, even that conference call where I hid under his desk, and my body still responds to him like it's the first time. Shit, am I falling for my boss? That's such a terrible idea it's not even funny.

"Should I be?" I fidget with my clutch, remembering yesterday when he bent me over the bathroom sink during lunch. My pussy buzzes with the memory.

"The Dixon Group is considering a major partnership." He adjusts his cufflinks. It's a tell of his that I've learned means he's making a decision. "Tonight is about building trust. Showing them who we are."

I nod, trying to focus on business instead of the way his thigh presses against mine in the back seat.

"You're quiet," Gabriel observes, his thumb tracing circles on my knee.

"Just thinking," I admit. "About us. About...what we're doing."

His eyes find mine in the dim light of the car. "Having second thoughts?"

"No! God, no. The opposite, actually."

I can't tell him I'm confusing mind-blowing sex with actual feelings. That would be humiliating. I'm such a cliché: the assistant falling for her powerful boss. But it feels like more than just fucking. The way he touches me when no one's watching, the private smiles only I see...the constant breeding dirty talk that blurs the line of what this is.

"I just don't want to mess this up." It's the truth, even if it's not the whole truth.

"You won't. We went over everything, and you'll do great."

His hand slides higher on my thigh. I'm reeling from confusion around Gabriel, and it's difficult to think about dinner. Is this just lust? Or am I actually falling in love with Gabriel Reed? And holy fuck, what am I supposed to do about it if I am?

As if he can tell I'm freaking out, he says, "Relax. Tonight is about having fun."

"And?" I prompt, sensing there's more.

Gabriel reaches into his jacket pocket and produces a small black box. "Consider this a test of your composure."

My stomach drops. The box is sleek, expensive, and about the size of jewelry packaging. But the heat in his eyes tells me this isn't jewelry.

"Sir, what is that?"

He opens the box. Inside, nestled in black silk, sits a small silver bullet and a remote. It's elegant, discreet, unmistakably designed for one specific use.

"You want me to…" I can't finish.

"I want you to wear this during dinner," Gabriel says, and his commanding tone makes butterflies swirl in my stomach. "While we get to know Mr. Dixon and his team."

My head spins. Is he serious? A business dinner with a remote-controlled vibrator? "The risk…"

"It is minimal if you maintain control." His fingers trace my jawline. "Which you will." He closes the box and takes my clutch, slipping the toy into it before handing it back to me. "But first, what's your safe word if things get too intense?"

"Red," I say, steadier than I expected. "Yellow to slow down."

"Use them without hesitation," he says, thumb brushing my lip. "Text me if you can't say it."

The valet opens my door, and my entire body trembles as Gabriel helps me out. This is going to be such delicious torture.

The Ivory Room's interior is stunning with soaring ceilings, soft lighting, and pristine white tablecloths. There's a quiet hum of conversation while people discuss things like yacht purchases. I feel out of place, since I'm still celebrating when my student loan payment clears without over-drafting.

"Ladies' room," I whisper urgently.

Gabriel nods toward a hallway. "Take your time. Make sure you get my gift positioned perfectly."

Am I really going to sit through dinner with a vibrator inside me while Gabriel controls it remotely?

Yes, yes, I am. I'm such a slut for this man.

My body tingles as I slide the device into place. It settles snugly, barely noticeable until I move, and then it shifts against sensitive spots. Imagining what it will feel like when it's turned on makes my pussy throb with anticipation.

Gabriel is waiting outside, leaning against the wall. His eyes sparkle with mischief. "Better?"

"We'll see," I manage.

My heart races as Gabriel's palm settles possessively on my lower back. The maître d' leads us to a private dining room with a table set for five. It's separated by frosted glass that creates an intimate space. There's fresh orchids and floor-to-ceiling windows with a stunning view of the city.

"Your party has arrived," the maître d' announces as three people enter—two men and a woman, all dressed in expensive but slightly flashy attire that screams Texas money.

Gabriel steps forward with his hand extended. "Jack, good to see you again."

Jack Dixon is tall with silver hair and a tan that suggests more time on golf courses than in boardrooms. His handshake is firm, borderline aggressive. "Gabriel Reed! Damn fine to be in New York. This place is something else."

I introduce myself, extending my hand. "Maya Williams, Mr. Reed's executive assistant."

Jack takes my hand and holds it a beat too long. "Well now, Gabriel didn't mention his assistant was such a pretty little thing."

I force a smile while my feminist brain screams. "I also handle client relations and legal research."

"Smart and beautiful," Jack says with a wink. "And please, call me Jack. Mr. Dixon was my daddy. This is my son, Travis," he continues, gesturing to a younger version of himself who is maybe in his early thirties, with the same confident swagger but a more modern suit. "And our legal counsel, Melissa Harding."

Melissa is sharp-eyed and perfectly polished, her blonde hair in a sleek bob. She gives me a knowing look that says she's dealt with Jack's good ol' boy routine for years.

"Let's sit, shall we?" Gabriel suggests, his hand returning to my lower back.

As we settle into our seats, Jack launches into a story about his flight. "I told the pilot to land this thing no matter what the tower said. We had reservations, for Christ's sake!"

I'm pretty sure that's not how air traffic control works, but I nod along.

Gabriel hasn't turned on the bullet toy. Maybe he's waiting until later?

As soon as I take a sip of water, the vibration starts low. I grip my water glass more tightly, fighting to keep my expression neutral as the sommelier discusses wine pairings. Gabriel orders without consulting the list while the vibration increases slightly. He has one hand in his pocket, obviously controlling the remote.

"New York treating you well?" Gabriel begins, voice professional while he occasionally glances my way.

The vibration pulses once, harder, before settling back to a gentle hum. I struggle to focus while wetness pools between my legs.

"Everything here is bigger than I expected," Jack responds with a laugh. "And I'm from Texas, so that's saying something!"

"Maya grew up here," Gabriel says, and the vibration shifts to a new pattern that makes my thighs clench. "She understands both the opportunities and challenges the city presents."

"Really?" Travis leans forward with interest. "What neighborhood?"

"Alphabet City," I manage, fighting the sensation building inside me. "The real New York—bodegas on every corner, basement apartments with questionable plumbing, neighbors who've lived there for decades."

"Fascinating," Jack says. "We're all about space in Texas. Can't imagine living in one of those shoebox apartments."

The vibration pulses harder, and I squeeze my thighs under the table. "The struggle taught me to work hard for everything."

Travis nods appreciatively, his eyes lingering on me a little too long. "I respect that. Too many people in our circle were born on third base thinking they hit a triple."

Gabriel's slight smile tells me he's pleased with me. The vibration shifts to a more intense pattern, more demanding. I reach for my wineglass, grateful for something to do with my hands.

"So, how's the oil business these days?" I ask, proud of how steady my voice sounds despite the chaos between my legs.

"Booming," Jack says, gesturing expansively. "But we're diversifying. Clean energy, tech investments. That's where Travis comes in. My boy's got a Harvard MBA and ideas that make my head spin."

"Dad still thinks the internet is a fad," Travis jokes, and everyone laughs.

As they speak about the family business, the vibration increases dramatically. I gasp softly, covering it with reaching for my napkin.

"You all right, darlin'?" Jack asks with concern.

"Fine," I manage. "Just this wine is stronger than I expected."

Gabriel's eyes flash with amusement as he decreases the intensity slightly. The conversation flows naturally and I listen to stories about the ranch, the differences between New York and Dallas, experiences of building a family business. I force myself to contribute. My pussy spasms rhythmically as Gabriel varies the patterns. Sometimes they're gentle waves, or sometimes they're sharp pulses that make my breath catch.

"Gabriel mentioned you're fresh out of school?" Melissa asks, speaking up for the first time.

"I recently graduated," I confirm, voice slightly breathless as Gabriel changes the pattern again. "I went to school during the day and worked at night to get through a double major in business administration and legal studies."

"Admirable," Melissa says with genuine respect. "Balancing work and education requires discipline."

If only she knew what kind of discipline I'm balancing right now.

The first course arrives and my mouth waters. It's a lobster bisque that's delicious, but it's almost impossible to eat while Gabriel continues messing with the toy settings.

"Gabriel, tell us about your expansion plans," Jack says between enthusiastic spoonfuls.

"Growth is essential," Gabriel responds, increasing the vibration just as I take a sip of wine. "But sustainable growth requires the right partnerships."

I nearly choke, covering it with a delicate cough. Gabriel's slight smile tells me he timed that perfectly.

"Partnership is about more than business terms," I add when I can speak again, surprised by my boldness. "It's about shared values and mutual respect."

"Exactly!" Jack agrees, slapping the table. "Too many firms just want to extract value and run. We're in it for the long haul."

The vibration shifts to something that targets exactly the right spot, making my pussy clench desperately around the device. I grip my napkin in my lap, fighting the urge to arch into the sensation. They continue discussing business practices while I sit there fighting not to moan.

"In Texas, a handshake means something," Jack explains. "My daddy taught me your word is your bond."

"That's refreshing," I manage, voice tight with the effort of maintaining control. "Integrity matters."

"You bet your ass it does," he beams. "This one gets it, Gabriel."

The main course arrives—a seared halibut with some sort of fancy lemon sauce. The server describes each element while I try to look interested instead of desperately aroused.

As we eat, the vibration shifts again, gentler but still driving me crazy. My legs shake beneath the table as pressure builds relentlessly. I'm close, so close, pleasure coiling tight in my core. I'm fighting the orgasm with everything I have.

Then the toy dies down to what I assume is the lowest setting while I vibrate with unfulfilled need. Gabriel's eyes hold mine, and his message is clear—not here, but soon.

I sit there trembling with frustrated arousal while the conversation continues with stories about Texas, questions about New York culture, and shared laughter over regional differences.

"I knew your father," Jack says to Gabriel unexpectedly.

The vibration stops abruptly. Something shutters behind Gabriel's eyes.

"My father had limited vision regarding certain opportunities," he says after a moment, voice controlled but there's a hardness in his tone. "The firm's current direction reflects integrity and a more progressive approach."

I glance between Gabriel and Jack, sensing history I don't understand.

Jack studies Gabriel for a long moment, then nods once. "Good. Your daddy was a shark, and not the kind you want to do business with. Glad to hear you're cutting your own path."

Gabriel smiles, and just like that, the tension dissipates. Gabriel restarts the vibration. It's gentle at first, then building steadily as conversation returns to lighter topics.

By the time our dark chocolate fondant with espresso gelato dessert is finished, I can barely focus and my pussy aches with frustration.

"This has been a wonderful evening," Gabriel says. "We should schedule a meeting to discuss specifics."

This dinner needs to end. I'm about ready to orgasm, and Gabriel knows it. The device pulses in a pattern that hits every sensitive spot, building pressure that demands release.

"Ms. Williams," Jack says, and I force myself to pay attention to his words instead of the pleasure between my legs. "We'd like you to be part of these discussions. Your perspective would be valuable."

"I'll be there," I manage.

Gabriel increases the intensity one final time, and I shift in my seat as I almost explode.

Then the vibration stops completely.

"Excellent evening," Jack says, rising to shake hands. "We look forward to building something meaningful together."

I stand on unsteady legs. "It was nice meeting you all."

Gabriel handles final pleasantries while I compose myself. The moment the Texans leave, he turns to me.

"Car. Now."

When we exit the restaurant, the night air is cool against my flushed skin. The Audi appears instantly, the driver opening the doors without being signaled. The privacy screen rises the moment we're inside.

"We're going to my place. I need to fuck you," Gabriel says as the car glides into traffic.

"Yes, sir," I sigh in happiness. Halle-fucking-lujah. "You know, you almost made me orgasm."

"But you didn't." He traces my thigh through the silk of my dress. "That dinner secured their trust. They'll sign with us."

"Because you impressed them," I say, moaning softly as he slides his hand beneath my dress.

"Because *we* impressed them," he corrects as his fingers brush against the soaked fabric of my panties.

I spread my legs, and my head falls back against leather as his fingers circle my clit through my panties. "Gabriel—sir—please. I need..."

"I know exactly what you need. And you'll get it soon."

He withdraws his hand, leaving me aching and empty as the car turns onto the West Side Highway. Lights from Hudson River Park streak past the window.

"Tell me about your apartment," Gabriel says unexpectedly.

"What?" The question catches me off guard, and my mind struggles to shift from arousal to conversation.

"Your apartment. What's it like?"

"It's…functional. Small. Basement level, so I get the occasional flooding when it rains hard." I give him a cheeky grin. "But maybe I can move soon with my new swanky job."

"And before this job? How did you manage?"

"My two part-time jobs," I admit, wondering where this is going. "Waitressing weekends at a diner in the East Village, barista work during the week in the evenings. It was enough to cover rent and ramen."

Gabriel's jaw tightens. "And tonight? Sitting in a restaurant where a bottle of wine costs more than your weekly budget?"

"Surreal," I confess. "Like I'm playing dress-up in someone else's life. I keep waiting for someone to realize I don't belong."

"But you do belong. With me."

As the car slows down, I want to believe him, but it's difficult to think about anything but getting his cock inside me.

His building is a converted warehouse with a discreet entrance. As soon as the car stops, a doorman appears instantly to open Gabriel's door.

I've never been here before, and I'm curious to see where he lives. The toy shifts inside me with every movement, and I try not to moan as we step into a private elevator.

The elevator opens directly into his penthouse, and Gabriel's control finally cracks. He presses me against the wall as his mouth claims mine with desperate hunger. My head spins with lust as he works the zipper on my dress.

The dress pools at my feet, leaving me in just my bra, panties, and heels in the marble foyer. The floor-to-ceiling windows showcase the glittering skyline.

He lifts me easily, and I wrap my legs around his waist as he carries me toward his bedroom. When he tosses me onto the bed, I giggle as I bounce on his soft mattress. I sober up quickly as I watch him unbutton his shirt. When he's undressed fully, he pulls me to the edge of the bed and slides my panties down my legs.

"The toy..." I groan.

"Stays exactly where it is," he says, voice dropping to that commanding tone that makes me want to obey him. "We're far from finished."

He pushes me back onto the bed and kisses me again with bruising intensity.

"You've earned your reward." He trails kisses down my neck. "Now I'm going to make you come and breed you until you can't remember your own name."

The remote appears in his grasp, and the vibration starts again. They're harder, faster, and more demanding than anything in the restaurant. My back arches off the bed as sensation overwhelms me.

The pleasure builds too quickly. "Sir, I can't..."

"You can." He moves his free hand to my breast and pulls on my nipple. "Come for me, Maya. Now."

The orgasm hits me like lightning, radiating outward from my core in waves of intense pleasure. I cry out, my body convulsing in pure bliss.

Before I can recover, Gabriel's mouth is between my legs. His tongue finds my clit while the toy continues pulsating inside me. The dual sensation pushes me immediately toward another peak, and my legs tremble uncontrollably.

"I can't. Not again so soon." I babble, fisting the sheets.

"You will," Gabriel insists, voice rough with desire.

The second orgasm crashes through me harder than the first, leaving me gasping and incoherent.

He rolls me onto my stomach and pulls my hips up, positioning me on my knees. I struggle to stay upright with boneless limbs. The toy shifts inside me, still vibrating gently. He pulls it out and positions it against my clit.

"This is what happens when you please me," he says, sinking his cock into me slowly. The dual pleasure of his cock and the vibration on my clit is almost too much. "When you excel. When you show everyone exactly why you belong in my world."

My arms give out, and my face smashes into his silk sheets as Gabriel drills into me. My head spins from pleasure as the vibrations of the toy and his cock hitting the perfect spot make me mindless.

Gabriel slams into me repeatedly. "Tell me you're mine."

"I'm yours. Completely yours."

Deep in my soul, I know it's true. I'd follow Gabriel anywhere.

"Mine to protect," he growls as he fucks me. "Mine to pleasure. Mine to breed."

The possessiveness in his voice pushes me over the edge again. My vision blurs as rapture skyrockets me to another plane of existence. I'm existing as pure energy as pleasure ripples from my fingertips to my toes.

I hear Gabriel groan from far away as he whacks against me one last time and unloads. I'm shivering with aftershocks as he fills me with his cum before collapsing beside me.

I'm not sure how long my face is smooshed into the bedding before I roll over to face him. "That was—I can't even—my brain is…"

He pulls me against his chest and kisses my temple. "Just enjoy the moment."

We lie tangled as our breathing slows, and Gabriel reaches between my legs, gently removing the bullet toy.

I giggle as I think about how I wore that throughout dinner. Six months ago, I never would have thought I'd be brave enough to do that, but Gabriel brings out the filthiest side of me. And now that I've met her, I'm never going back to who I was before.

Gabriel kisses me softly. "Stay with me tonight, my giggly girl."

I squint up at him. "You want that?"

"Yes." Something vulnerable flickers in his eyes.

It's not a command this time. It's a request. Maybe even a need.

"I'll stay."

As I curl against him, a sense of rightness settles over me. This isn't about him being my boss or dom. This is about becoming exactly who I was always meant to be.

CHAPTER 9

The next Saturday, after Gabriel spends the morning sending me filthy texts about everything he's imagining doing to me, he invites me to spend the night again. As I'm riding the elevator to his penthouse, my phone pings with a text.

Unknown number:

> Be careful. His last assistant who visited the penthouse filed for a transfer the next day. Ask about the locked room – C.

My stomach twists with irritation. I'm getting sick of Cameron and his insinuations. But what locked room? I slip my phone into my purse, trying to tamp down my curiosity. I refuse to play into Cameron's bullshit.

Gabriel meets me when I step out of the elevator. He's looking devastating in charcoal slacks and a crisp white shirt with rolled-up sleeves that showcase his forearms. My pussy buzzes just looking at him.

"Glad you wanted to come," he says and kisses me softly.

"After all those texts this morning, did you think I wouldn't?" I slip off my coat and eye him. He looks like he's been at work or in a meeting. "Is everything okay? Did something happen with the Morrison deal?"

"Everything is fine. Tonight isn't about work."

My body tingles with anticipation. It's been a long week, so I'm down with forgetting about work. But something is different. Gabriel's jaw is tight, and I can sense he's wound up.

"What's wrong?" I ask, following him into the living room.

"Cameron cornered a paralegal yesterday," Gabriel says, pouring two glasses of wine. "Tried to pressure her to have drinks after work."

"What happened?" My stomach tightens as Gabriel hands me a glass.

"She reported it to HR, but the senior partners are resistant to formal action without more substantial evidence. I've been tracking what Cameron does and collecting statements. This needs to stop."

I listen with concern as Gabriel explains the situation with Cameron. This is exactly the predatory behavior that makes workplaces toxic for women.

"That's awful," I say, genuinely troubled. "I'm glad she reported it. Do you need any help gathering evidence? I could talk to some of the other assistants discreetly."

Gabriel looks surprised but appreciative of my offer. "Thank you. I might take you up on that."

The text from Cameron burns in my mind, but I can't bring myself to mention it. Not when Gabriel is already this wound up about the situation. Besides, Cameron's cryptic warnings about locked rooms and former assistants sound more like manipulation tactics than actual evidence. If I'm going to help Gabriel build a case, it needs to be with real, substantiated proof—not whatever games Cameron is playing.

I take a sip of wine to calm my nerves. As much as I care about stopping Cameron, I can tell Gabriel needs a break from work stress tonight.

"But you said tonight isn't about work," I remind him gently, touching his arm. "And I'm guessing there's something else on your mind?"

"Come with me," he says, his expression softening. "There's something I need to show you."

I follow him past his bedroom, and we approach a door I've noticed before but never seen opened. Heavy. Dark wood. A lock that requires an actual key.

If I didn't trust him so much by now, the secrecy might concern me, but I'm still a little nervous, so I joke, "Are you about to show me the skeletons in your closet? Because I'm not sure I packed my running shoes."

Gabriel stops and pulls a key from his pocket. "This is something I've been wanting to show you. But only if you're ready."

Ready for what? "Gabriel—"

"Sir," he corrects.

Huh, okay, so this is how it is.

"Sir, what's behind that door?" This better not be the moment I find out he's not as great as I've been thinking all this time.

Instead of answering, he unlocks the door and steps aside. "See for yourself."

I step through the doorway and freeze. Holy fuck.

The room looks nothing like the rest of his sophisticated penthouse. It has dark burgundy walls, and soft, recessed lighting creates pools of warmth. The equipment in the room makes my brain blank because I have no idea what half of it is supposed to do.

A leather bench sits in the center with restraint attachments. Chains hang from reinforced ceiling points. An entire wall displays implements—floggers, paddles, cuffs in various materials from leather to silk. There's a bed in the corner with red sheets.

The air smells of leather and sandalwood, which is different than the rest of his condo. The floor seems to be some kind of laminate that would wipe clean easily.

"Jesus Christ," I breathe. "This is like something out of a movie, except way more intimidating and—"

"Maya." Gabriel's voice stops me.

"What?" I don't know what to think, and my hands are shaking as I stare at the bench. I think someone rests on it to get spanked. What would that feel like?

"This is the part of me you haven't met yet."

He places his hands on my shoulders, and I lean back against his chest because my legs feel unsteady. I don't know what to think, but the bench intrigues me.

"Cameron sent me a text," I blurt out. "He mentioned a locked room. This is what he was talking about, isn't it?"

Gabriel tenses. "What text?"

"He texted me right as I got here. He said your last assistant who visited this room filed for a transfer the next day."

Gabriel tightens his grip on my shoulders. "Jessica asked for the transfer to Chicago after Cameron threatened to release photos of her leaving my building. She was never in this room."

"So he's lying." I'm not surprised.

"Cameron's default mode is lies." Gabriel wraps his arms around me and rests his chin on my head. "I've never brought a personal assistant in here before."

The room isn't new, and I doubt he has it just for show. "But you've brought subs in here."

"Yes. But not like this. Not with someone who matters."

Someone who matters. My body tingles even as my mind races with questions.

"If you've never brought an assistant here before, how does Cameron even know it exists?"

"Cameron poached one of my casual play partners after we ended things. She told him about the room. I didn't see how he could use the information against me."

"Of course he would figure out a way," I mutter, anger flaring. "He's a fucking snake."

"Yes, but he won't win. Not this time. I've got plans to take care of him. But I don't want him to ruin our night."

This dungeon room is a lot to process. But it feels right. Like a piece of him I've been waiting to see.

"So," I say, turning in his arms to face him. "This is you. This is us now."

His eyes search mine. "Only if you want it to be. You decide. You're in control here."

I reach up and cup his jaw. "I want it. I want you. All of you."

He kisses me deeply, and my toes curl. My entire body lights up with desire as his tongue twines with mine. When he pulls back, his voice is rough. "Then let's begin."

He releases me, and I study the room again. The leather bench, the chains, the implements on the wall. It's intimidating, but it also gives me a thrilling sense of adventure.

"What are those?" I point to the leather cuffs hanging from a hook. "And that thing that looks like an X? And—oh God, is that what I think it is?" I'm rambling again.

Gabriel smiles slightly. "Those are restraints. That's a St. Andrew's cross. And yes, that's exactly what you think it is."

Maya from just two months ago probably would have run scared, but Maya today is curious about everything in the room and getting wetter by the second while staring at a wall of mysterious implements.

"Why show me this now?" I ask.

There's a vulnerability in his eyes, flickering beneath his control. "Because I need you to understand all of me. Not just the man in the office."

This isn't just about kinky sex. This is Gabriel showing me something fundamental about himself.

"What would we do in here?" I ask, though I've read enough books and watched enough movies to have a pretty good idea.

"Whatever you consent to. Whatever we want to explore together."

I meet his gaze. The intensity there steals my breath. It's not just desire, but something deeper like he wants to corrupt and protect me at the same time.

"Before we go further," Gabriel says, his voice dropping lower, "we need clear boundaries. This only works with complete trust. You told me you don't like pain."

I imagine him bending me over the padded bench. My pussy throbs with need as I picture his hand coming down on my ass. "Well...what if I was willing to try a little pain?"

Gabriel's eyes glimmer with lust. "That can be arranged. What else?"

"No humiliation," I say firmly. "I like being a slut or your fucktoy, but I don't want anything harsher."

I didn't realize I even felt that way until I said it. Look at me being assertive. Go me.

"Good. What about restraints? Being tied down or immobilized?"

A flush warms me at the question. My ex-boyfriend tied me to the bed a couple of times and blindfolded me. It was mostly just fun and nothing intense, but I enjoyed it. "That seems...that's a yes."

"And impact play? Being spanked or flogged?"

I'm getting wetter just from him asking me what I want. I shift my weight from one foot to the other. "I don't know about flogging. Maybe start gentle and see?"

"Perfect." Gabriel smiles, and the twinkle in his eye tells me he's imagining doing all those things to me. "And you will use your safe words if you need to."

"Promise. Red, yellow, and green," I repeat.

He swoops down and kisses me, and I hum against his mouth in pleasure.

"Now," Gabriel says, stepping back. "Remove your clothes."

"All of them?" I'm suddenly aware of how exposed I'll be in this strange room.

"All of them." His voice leaves no room for negotiation. "I want to see every inch of what belongs to me."

My hands shake as I pull my shirt over my head. I fumble with my bra clasp and have to force myself to calm down. My jeans hit the floor, followed by my panties. Standing naked in his playroom is different from being undressed in his bedroom; I immediately feel more vulnerable.

"Beautiful," Gabriel murmurs. "Absolutely beautiful."

My skin flushes. I cross my arms instinctively, then force myself to drop them.

"What now?" I ask, trying not to fidget.

"Now you learn what it means to truly submit to me." He moves to the wall, selecting a leather paddle. "Position yourself over the bench."

Oh God, how did he know I wanted to be spanked more than anything else? My legs wobble as I approach the padded surface. "Like, how exactly? Because this thing doesn't come with instructions, and I don't want to do it wrong."

"Your knees go on the lower ledge, and you rest against the upper one. There are bars you can hold on to on the far side."

Seems easy enough when he explains it. The leather is soft against my stomach as I lean forward, my ass tilted up, hands braced for support. My pussy throbs with anticipation.

"Good girl," Gabriel says, and those two words send a zip of pleasure through me.

There's an odd sense of freedom from putting myself in this position. He didn't just bend me over and wait for me to say no if I didn't want it. I am choosing this.

He stands behind me, one hand on my lower back. "This is about trust. About letting go of the control you cling to everywhere else."

His hand cups my ass, fingers tracing patterns that make me arch into his touch. My pussy clenches around nothing, desperate to be filled.

"Do you trust me?" he asks.

"Yes, sir," I whisper, and I mean it.

The first strike is barely a tap and gentle.

"That's it?" I blurt out, then flush. "Sorry, I didn't mean—it just surprised me. It doesn't hurt, it's just different."

"Breathe," Gabriel commands. "Let yourself feel everything."

The second strike is firmer. A tingle spreads from my ass, running down my thighs and up my spine.

Gabriel strokes my spine. "How does that feel?"

"Weird," I admit. "But not bad weird."

As he continues to spank me, the constant chatter and worry in my head fades under the rhythmic impact. Each slap sends a jolt straight to my clit, and I push back, wanting more.

"Ohhhh," I breathe. "I think I see why people do this."

Gabriel laughs as the strikes come faster. Desire threatens to consume me with each impact, arousal mixing with the sharp sensation. I can't think about anything but what he's doing to me. My nipples tighten against the leather bench, and I'm so wet I can feel it dripping down my thighs.

"My fucktoy enjoys her spanking."

Mmm, yes, yes I do.

He slides his fingers between my legs. When he circles my clit, I nearly sob with relief. Pressure builds low in my belly from the combination of the sting on my ass and his fingers creating magic between my legs.

"Please," I gasp.

"Please what?" Gabriel sounds maddeningly calm.

I struggle for words. "Please make me come."

"Not yet, my sweet slut. We're just beginning." He withdraws his hand, and I whimper. Gabriel returns with silk scarves. "Wrists behind your back."

My pulse pounds as I do as he commands.

"I'm restraining you," he says as he secures the silk around my wrists efficiently, "so you can't do anything except feel."

The restraints are soft but secure. I test them and realize I can't break free. A delicious helplessness washes over me, and I love it.

"Still good?" Gabriel asks.

"Yes, green," I answer, knowing it's true.

"Good girl."

He moves behind me again, and I hear the whisper of fabric. When his hands return, they're covered in something smooth that amplifies every touch.

"What are you wearing?" I ask, trying to see.

"Silk gloves," Gabriel explains as he traces paths across my back, sides, and ass.

The silk creates friction that's both soothing and arousing. Each touch from him lights up nerve endings I didn't know I had. When he trails his fingers down my spine, I shiver and wish he were fucking me.

One of his hands slides between my legs again, and I can tell he's removed the glove as he rubs circles around my clit. I pull against the restraints instinctively, wanting to touch him back, but the bindings hold firm.

"This is what you need," Gabriel says, his fingers working me into a frenzy. "To let go completely."

My orgasm quickly builds, the restraints forcing me to simply experience the pleasure. Tension coils more and more tightly in my core, my legs trembling as I teeter on the edge.

I gasp, "I can't. It's too much."

"Be a good girl and come for me."

The climax hits me like lightning, radiating outward in waves. I cry out and convulse as Gabriel works me through every spike of bliss. My pussy spasms wildly, clenching around nothing as pleasure crashes through me so intensely I see stars.

"What was that? That was...I've never..." I sob, my legs trembling.

"Good girl," Gabriel murmurs, stroking my back as I come down.

My legs feel like jelly as he unties my wrists, massaging the feeling back into my hands before helping me stand. I lean against his chest, still processing. My body buzzes with aftershocks, little ripples of pleasure still running through me.

"How do you feel?" he asks.

"Good, but is it always like that?"

"Like what?"

"My mind just went quiet for the first time in my life." I meet his gaze. "I didn't know that was possible."

Gabriel smiles in response, and my heart flutters.

A thought pops into my head, but I hesitate before voicing it because I don't want to sound stupid. "So this isn't just about the office stuff. About playing games during work hours?"

His arms tighten around me. "No, it's not."

"I want to explore more," I say, and give him my sexiest grin.

Gabriel kisses me deeply, and my body buzzes in pleasure despite the intense orgasm I just had.

When we break apart, he rests his forehead against mine. "Are you sure?"

"I'm more turned on than I've ever been in my life, so I think that's a yes."

He laughs warmly. "Then we'll explore everything together. Every limit, every desire, every fantasy you have."

"Starting now?"

He eyes me with a predatory hunger. "Oh, yeah. Ready for round two?"

"Yep, bring it on."

Gabriel's eyes twinkle and he gives me another quick kiss before selecting something from the wall. He returns with soft, red rope that looks both beautiful and intimidating. "Let's see how you like this."

"Yes, sir."

The first touch of rope against my skin sends electricity through me. Gabriel works with precision. The rope hugs my body, crosses between my breasts, wraps around my thighs. Each loop and knot increases the pressure in subtle, delicious ways that make my skin sing.

"This is called shibari," he explains. "Japanese rope bondage."

With each pass of the rope, I sink deeper into a fuzzy mental space and my thoughts quiet. All that exists is the sensation of rope and Gabriel's hands.

"Look at yourself," he murmurs after securing the last knot.

He turns me toward a mirror on the wall, and my lips part in surprise. The red rope creates an intricate pattern across my body, framing my breasts, highlighting my hips, making me look like erotic art.

"Holy fuck," I breathe. "Is that really me?"

"That's you."

As he guides me to the bench again, positioning me on my knees, I understand. This version of myself was always inside me. I just never had anyone to help me explore.

Gabriel unzips his pants. "Ready for more?"

I look over my shoulder, more certain than I've ever been. "Yes, sir. I'm ready for everything."

Even if I don't know what "everything" means yet.

Gabriel positions his cock at my pussy. I'm so wet that he sinks in easily. My pussy stretches around him, welcoming him home.

He groans, "Time to use my fucktoy."

Gabriel picks up speed, drilling into me as pressure builds low in my belly. My pussy grips his cock eagerly while pleasure builds rapidly at my core.

He pulls on the rope with each thrust. Soon, I'm back at that point where everything is too much but also exactly what I need. My clit throbs desperately, and each time he bottoms out, it sends shockwaves of pleasure through me.

"Sir," I whimper as pleasure spirals through me, "I can't."

"Yes, you can." Gabriel fucks me harder, and his cock hits exactly the right spot inside me. "Let go."

When my climax breaks, I cry out, "Oooh, fuck!"

Wave after wave of pleasure rips through me. I spasm around him rhythmically, milking his cock as the orgasm seems to go on forever. All I can do is take his cock for as long as he wants to fuck me.

My brain shuts off, and it barely registers when he groans and shudders against me as he unloads deep inside my pussy. The warm spurt of his cum triggers another smaller orgasm that leaves me shaking.

By the time I come down, tears are streaming down my face.

"Are you okay?" Gabriel's voice is concerned as he pulls me off the bench and releases the ropes. He massages me, searching for injury.

I take a moment to find words, but finally, they emerge on a breathy sob. "I'm good. That was amazing."

Gabriel holds me, and I cling to him as I let myself process. His cum drips down my thighs, but I'm too blissed out to care.

"God, what did you just do to me?" I can't seem to stop crying, and Gabriel strokes my back soothingly.

"Showed you that you're capable of more pleasure than you thought."

Yeah, something like that.

He picks me up and carries me to bed, leaving me briefly to open a mini-fridge over by a counter and sink. He comes back with water and turkey sandwiches. Yep, he totally planned all of this.

We sit on the bed and eat together. The post-orgasmic haze makes me feel giddy.

"My mom would have hated this place," I say suddenly, surprising myself.

Gabriel pauses mid-bite. "Your mother?"

I nod, staring off into space and imagine exactly what my mother would've said. "She was big on independence. 'Never need a man for anything, Maya.' That was her mantra after my dad left when I was seven."

"Tell me about her," Gabriel says softly, setting his sandwich aside.

"She worked three jobs sometimes. Cleaning houses during the day, bartending at night, weekend shifts at a laundromat." My throat tightens. "When I was in high school, I started working too. We had this system where I'd leave my tips in this ceramic frog on the kitchen counter, and she'd leave hers. Whoever had the better night would slip a little extra into the other's pile when they weren't looking."

Gabriel's hand finds mine. "She sounds remarkable."

"She was. She got sick my sophomore year of college with aggressive breast cancer. That's why I had to leave that internship at Jackson & Klein. I couldn't work unpaid while she needed care." I swallow hard. "She died the summer before my senior year. The medical bills wiped out everything."

"I'm sorry, I had no idea."

"I didn't want you to know. Didn't want to be the sad charity case." I meet his eyes. "But I'm telling you now because...because I think she would have loved that I'm making my own decisions about what I want."

Gabriel pulls me against his chest. "Thank you for telling me."

"It's weird. When I was tied up like that, when I surrendered, it's the only time my brain's ever shut off. I wasn't worrying about bills or feeling guilty that I couldn't save her."

"That's what submission can do."

I laugh softly. "Yeah, my therapist would have a field day with that."

"You don't have a therapist."

"Haven't found one yet now that I can afford one, so instead, I'm letting hot dom guys tie me up."

Gabriel tilts my chin up. "Not just any dom guy."

"No," I agree, feeling suddenly shy. "Not just any dom."

I take another bite of my sandwich and study Gabriel, suddenly curious about something I've never asked. "You know, I've been wondering...what were you even doing on that subway that night we met? You don't exactly seem like the public transportation type with your fancy cars and drivers." I tease him with a smile.

"Sometimes I ride the subway when I need to think and clear my head," he admits. "The anonymity helps. No one knows who I am, no one wants anything from me. It's just...simpler." He pauses, his thumb tracing circles on my knee. "That night, I'd been dealing with Cameron's latest sabotage attempt and needed space from everything. Then I saw you, and suddenly I wasn't thinking about work anymore."

My heart squeeze with happiness, and I lean over and kiss him. I'm glad I can make him forget work.

When we're done eating, we talk late into the night about life and what matters most to us. For the first time since I met him, it feels like he's allowing me all the way in. No more keeping parts of himself hidden from me behind locked doors.

As I drift toward sleep in Gabriel's arms, I realize it's no longer just a danger of me falling for him, I already have. And I'm not entirely sure that's a bad thing.

After breakfast the next morning, we snuggle on his couch in the living room and Gabriel's expression turns serious. "We need to talk about Cameron. There's something else you should know."

My morning-after post-orgasmic haze clears immediately. Nothing kills the afterglow like hearing that creep's name. "What about him?"

"When I said he threatened Jessica with photos, I didn't tell you why it mattered." Gabriel pulls me onto his lap. "Jessica was engaged to a politician's son. Her fiancé knew about me, and our relationship was consensual, but those photos would have destroyed her engagement and created a scandal for his parents."

"That's blackmail." And seriously fucked up. I knew Cameron was a snake, but this is next-level creepy.

"Yes. And it's why we agreed she should transfer to Chicago. To protect her." Gabriel's mouth forms a thin line. "Cameron doesn't just want what's mine. He wants to destroy anything I value."

"He's watching us," I say, remembering those creepy texts. "The messages, knowing when I visit your penthouse…"

Gabriel hugs me close. "Yes, which is why you need to be certain this is worth it."

I think about everything I've experienced since meeting Gabriel, and the sense of belonging I've never felt anywhere else. He pushes me to be more confident, and he makes me feel valued.

I give him a cheeky grin. "I'm sure. And luckily, I don't have any political aspirations. If he takes pictures of me leaving your building, the worst thing that happens is my landlord finds out I sometimes sleep somewhere that doesn't flood when it rains."

He laughs and gives me a thorough kiss that quickly turns into me on my back on the couch while he ravishes me.

Oh yeah, this is totally worth it.

CHAPTER 10

Two days later, I'm gathering my coat and purse at the end of the day when Gabriel's office door flies open. His composure is cracked, and his hair is slightly disheveled, as if he's been running his hands through it.

"Maya, I need you to stay." His voice carries an edge. "The Morrison acquisition is in jeopardy."

"What happened?"

"The FTC just issued a Second Request. We have twenty-four hours to produce our initial document production list, and they're demanding everything." Gabriel runs his hand through his hair again, messing it further. "If we don't get this right, the deal dies. We're talking about a $400 million acquisition and our biggest client relationship."

Fuck. "What do you need me to do?"

"Document review and privilege logging. We need to identify every responsive document in Morrison's files while protecting attorney-client privilege." He moves to his desk, already gathering his laptop. "Plus, we need to research recent FTC merger challenges in the telecommunications sector to anticipate their arguments."

I nod, my mind shifting into work mode. This is the moment that could make or break everything. The opportunity to prove I'm more than just a girl from Alphabet City who happened to land this job.

"Conference room or library?"

"Library. We'll need access to the secure document review platform." Gabriel loosens his tie slightly. "Maya, this will take all night. The client is flying in tomorrow morning expecting answers. Are you prepared for that?"

The way he says it makes my skin tingle. All night. Alone. In the law library. Jesus Christ, Maya. Focus on the work, not on how his voice makes your pussy throb.

"Yes, sir," I respond automatically, then flush when I realize we're still technically in work hours.

"Good. Gather your laptop and everything you need. I'll meet you in the library in ten minutes."

As I collect my stuff, my cellphone rings; another anonymous number.

Unknown Number:

> FTC moving fast on Morrison. Interesting how they knew exactly where to look. Good luck with the Second Request – C.

Cameron. Did he feed information to the FTC to sabotage Gabriel's deal?

My stomach churns as I head toward the library. Before I reach it, Gabriel joins me in the hallway, carrying a stack of files and his laptop bag.

A security guard nods at us as we pass him on the way to the library. "Working late tonight, Mr. Reed?"

"FTC Second Request," Gabriel responds grimly. "We'll be here until dawn."

The guard checks his watch. "Rough night. You'll see me on my rounds."

My pussy gives a little throb at the thought of being alone in the library for hours with Gabriel. That slut needs to understand we have work to do. Gabriel's career is on the line.

Once we're alone, I show Gabriel the text. "I think Cameron tipped off the FTC."

Gabriel's jaw tightens. "That would be highly unethical, but proving it would be nearly impossible. The FTC gets tips from competitors regularly."

"Can he really get away with that?"

"Only if we can't satisfy the Second Request properly." Gabriel's voice is steel. "Which we will. Cameron may play dirty, but we play better."

We settle at a table and dig into the research in the online databases. We work for the next hour, and I fidget with my pen, trying not to click it as I read briefs that would've been foreign to me two months ago. Now I understand the implications, the connections, the way these cases build on each other. My work experience and college degree are finally paying off.

Around 8:00, Gabriel looks up from his screen. "We should order food. This is going to be a marathon, not a sprint."

"I'm starving," I admit. "Thai? Italian?"

"Whatever keeps us sharp. You choose." He slides his phone toward me. "I trust your judgment."

Something warm blooms in my chest at those simple words. I order Thai from our favorite place. I get pad Thai for me, green curry for him, and spring rolls to share. The fact that I know his order by heart feels strangely intimate.

"Food will be here in forty minutes," I tell him, returning to a thread of emails between Morrison's CEO and their head of sales.

When the delivery arrives, the security guard brings it up to us. Gabriel signs for it and tips generously.

"You two need anything else?" the guard asks.

"We're good, thanks," Gabriel replies.

We clear a small space among our documents. Gabriel opens containers while I continue reviewing a particularly complex licensing agreement that might trigger additional FTC scrutiny.

"This is what I love about this work," Gabriel says, taking a bite while scanning a document. "High stakes with real consequences."

"Even when Cameron tries to sabotage us?"

"Especially then. It means we're doing something that matters." He passes me a document marked for potential privilege issues. "What's your read on this one?"

I review the email chain carefully. "Outside counsel is copied, so attorney-client privilege applies. But the business strategy discussion might still be responsive to Request 15."

"Agreed. We'll log it as privileged but note the responsive elements." Gabriel makes a note in the privilege log. "You're getting good at this analysis."

The compliment sends warmth through my chest, but I stay focused on the work. As the night goes on, it becomes increasingly difficult to concentrate. Every glance from Gabriel is like a physical touch. Every casual brush of his fingers when passing documents builds tension.

I cross and uncross my legs, a telltale sign of sexual frustration that I can't seem to control around him. My body is betraying me. I'm getting wet when we need to save this case.

At 11:30, Gabriel stands and stretches. "Coffee break?"

"I'll get it," I offer, needing distance before I do something inappropriate.

"No. We'll go together."

The break room is empty, and I lean against the counter while he uses the espresso machine. The thing has more buttons than a spaceship control panel, but Gabriel knows how to run it.

He hands me a cappuccino. "How are you holding up?"

"Fine," I lie, taking a sip to hide my face. I'm turned on and feeling a little tired. Neither of them is something I can do anything about right now. "Just focused on getting this done."

"You sure? You seem a little distracted. Are you wishing I'd slide my hands between your legs under the table like last time?"

My cheeks burn as my body hums with arousal. He's not making this easier for me. "Hey, I'm working."

"Are you?" He moves closer, pinning me against the counter. "Your breathing changes when I get close."

I quiver with anticipation as he cages me with his arms, hands braced on either side of the counter. "Sir, we have work to finish. We can't mess this up because we can't keep our hands off each other."

"We do have work." His thumb traces my jawline. "But we also have needs that require attention. Needs that help us think more clearly when satisfied."

A delicious ache between my legs roars to life. "But the security guard might walk in."

"He won't make rounds for a bit." Gabriel's mouth hovers inches from mine. "Plenty of time for what I have in mind."

"Time for what?" I whisper, though my body already knows the answer.

"For me to fuck your sweet pussy."

Yeah, I'm not going to stop him. When I don't put up any additional resistance, he kisses me with a desperate hunger. I melt into him, my hands fisting in his shirt as hours of building tension finally find release.

"We shouldn't," I murmur against his lips.

"Probably not," Gabriel agrees as he works the buttons on my blouse open. "But you're going to obey me anyway, aren't you?"

Jesus Christ, I love this. "Yes, sir."

Gabriel kisses down the column of my neck, nibbling on the sensitive spot that makes my knees weak. He slides his hands under my blouse, and I arch into his touch.

"We should go back to the library," I moan. The library is less likely to have someone walking in.

"Yes," Gabriel agrees, but he's already unfastening my bra. "We should."

Neither of us moves.

He brushes his thumbs across my nipples, and I have to force myself not to moan again.

"Maya." Gabriel groans. "Tell me to stop."

I meet his gaze, seeing my desperation reflected there. "I can't."

Gabriel lifts me onto the counter, pushes my skirt up around my waist, and rubs his hand over my panties. "So wet already. Were you thinking about my cock while we worked?"

"Yes," I admit breathlessly.

His fingers brush the fabric of my panties aside and he rubs my clit. I squeeze my eyes shut as pleasure radiates through my body.

"Look at me," Gabriel commands softly.

I force my eyes open, meeting his gaze as he works magic on my clit. The risk of discovery is hotter than I expected.

"We need to go back," I whisper, even as I spread my legs wider for him.

"We will after you come for me."

He slides two fingers into my pussy, and I slap my hand over my mouth to keep from crying out as he finger-fucks me.

Footsteps echo in the hallway.

Gabriel stills immediately, but he doesn't withdraw his hand. We both freeze, listening as the security guard's footsteps pass the break room and continue down the corridor.

"Fuck," I breathe when the sound fades.

"Indeed." Gabriel's slight smile is pure predator. "Library. Now."

He helps me down from the counter onto unsteady legs. My hands shake as I straighten my clothes while Gabriel adjusts his shirt.

"We really are insane," I mutter, following him back toward the library.

"Completely," Gabriel agrees. "And we're not stopping."

Gabriel leads me to the back corner of the library and presses me against the towering bookshelf. Leather-bound legal volumes dig into my spine as he pins me there with his body.

"Here?" I whisper, my eyes darting toward the library entrance, but we're hidden from view.

"Right the fuck here. I need you, and I'm not waiting," Gabriel growls, tearing at my blouse buttons. His fingers fumble in his haste. "Against these law books while I fuck my slut."

My pussy clenches at his filthy words. God, I love it when he's this desperate to fuck me.

He abandons my shirt, leaving it hanging open with my bra exposed.

"No more talking." His mouth crashes down on mine, his tongue invading as he shoves my skirt up around my waist. I gasp against his lips as his fingers dive beneath my panties and he rubs my clit.

"Your cock, I need it now," I whimper, rocking against his hand.

Gabriel removes his hand from my pussy long enough to free his thick cock. I lick my lips at the sight of the veins bulging along the shaft, and the swollen head already glistening.

"Look at you," he groans as he yanks my panties aside again. "My little office slut desperate to be fucked where anyone could walk in."

I love it when he gets rough like this. He lifts my leg up, and I wrap it around his thighs. When he slams his cock into my pussy in one brutal thrust, I cry out. The sound echoes off the high ceilings before I bite down on my lip.

"Fuck, so good," Gabriel groans as he drills into me. "Squeezing my cock like a perfect little fucktoy. Your pussy was made to take my cum. Made to be filled and bred by me."

He pounds into me with no finesse, just pure animal need driving each deep stroke. My tits bounce with every slam, my nipples hard peaks poking through my bra.

"Tell me," he grunts, his breath hot against my ear as he fucks me harder. "Tell me you love my cock destroying your greedy pussy."

"Yes!" I arch to take him deeper. "I love your cock, sir! Fill me up. Plant your seed deep inside me. I'm your slut, your fucktoy."

Footsteps echo from the library entrance. Fuck.

Gabriel freezes and clamps his hand over my mouth. "Quiet, unless you want the entire building to hear you getting bred."

His cock is still buried to the hilt inside me, and we both hold our breath.

"Mr. Reed?" the guard calls out. "Everything okay back there?"

"Just finishing research," Gabriel responds, his voice startlingly calm while his cock pulses inside me. My pussy clenches around him involuntarily, making him groan softly.

"All right then. I'll check back later."

We stay frozen until the footsteps fade. Gabriel doesn't waste a second. He withdraws almost completely before slamming back into me with enough force to make the bookshelf rattle.

"You fucking little tease," he growls, pounding into my sopping pussy. "Clenching around me while he was right there. You wanted him to find us, didn't you? Wanted him to see what a slut you are for my cock?"

"N-no!" But my traitorous pussy spasms around his shaft, betraying how much the danger turns me on.

He pistons into me faster. "Come for me. Right fucking now."

"I can't—" But my body doesn't agree with me. Pleasure detonates through every nerve. My scream is muffled against his shoulder as I convulse around his cock.

"Fucking take it!" Gabriel roars as he slams home one last time. Hot cum erupts inside me, jet after jet filling me as he grinds deep. "Take every fucking drop."

When he's done unloading, we sag against the bookshelf, both gasping. His cum leaks down my thighs, a filthy reminder of what we just did. Gabriel pulls out slowly, making me whimper at the sudden emptiness.

"You okay?" he rasps, tucking his softening cock away.

I lean into his warmth, still processing what just happened. "That was…"

"A very needed break," Gabriel finishes, and I giggle.

"I suppose I might be able to concentrate more easily now. Nothing like a library orgasm to clear the mind."

Gabriel watches me as I adjust my clothing and button my shirt. I can already feel his cum dripping onto the fabric of my panties.

"Back to work," he says, returning to his professional demeanor. "We have three hours until the filing deadline."

As we return to our research, I'm hyperaware of the dampness between my legs and of Gabriel's eyes occasionally finding mine.

The twinkle in his eye is our shared secret, and when he grins at me, a sudden realization hits me.

I love him.

Oh fuck. I stare blankly at my computer screen, and before I panic, I push the thought aside. I'll deal with that later.

To distract myself, I ask, "So how bad is this?"

"Manageable, if we're thorough. But there are some communications that are going to be difficult to explain." Gabriel sighs. "Morrison's executives weren't always careful about how they discussed potential competitive impacts."

"Anything that kills the deal?"

"Not necessarily. But the FTC will use certain emails to argue that Morrison intended to reduce competition. We need to contextualize everything properly."

I feel the weight of responsibility. "Gabriel. Thank you for trusting me with this level of responsibility."

There's something in his expression that makes my pulse skip. "You've earned it."

The praise means everything, but I push aside the personal feelings it stirs. We have work to finish.

Over the next several hours, we develop a rhythm. Gabriel handles the complex privilege determinations while I manage the broader document categorization. When we encounter problematic documents, we discuss strategy and potential client counseling.

Outside the conference room windows, the sky lightens with the first hints of dawn. At 6 a.m. Gabriel reviews our final privilege log and document production list.

"Ready to submit?" he asks.

I double-check our work one final time. "All requests are addressed, privilege log complete, production timeline established."

"Excellent." Gabriel initiates the secure upload to the FTC portal. "Maya, this was exceptional work. You handled this like a senior associate."

The compliment sends warmth through my exhausted body. "Thank you, sir. What happens next?"

"I present our preliminary findings to Morrison's board this afternoon, then begin the actual document production. The FTC will likely have follow-up questions, and we need to be prepared for potential depositions."

I yawn and suddenly realize something has shifted between us. This wasn't just an all-night work session—it was a test of whether we could function as partners under pressure.

As if he senses what I'm thinking, he pulls me to him. Something in his expression makes my pulse skip as he says, "This changes things between us."

"How?"

"Because now I know you'll follow me anywhere. Even into complete madness."

"I will," I admit. I'll risk everything for him.

Gabriel smiles. "Good. Just remember that when we're not exhausted, because I have plans for us."

As we gather our materials and prepare to submit the filing that will save the Morrison deal, I'm curious what those plans are, but I push aside the thought. "What do you think Cameron will do when he realizes his sabotage didn't work?" I ask as we walk toward the elevators.

"He'll try something else. But we can handle whatever he throws at us."

As we submit the Second Request response that will keep the Morrison acquisition alive, I realize that I'm so damn tired, but happy. This is exactly the kind of legal work I want to build my career on, and Gabriel is the man I want by my side.

Chapter 11

I'm organizing Gabriel's calendar when the elevator doors slide open. My head snaps up as Cameron Webb strides in. My stomach muscles tense as my body's warning system fires up.

"Maya Williams," he says, approaching my desk with a smile that doesn't reach his eyes. They stay cold, appraising me like I'm an asset to acquire. "Gabriel's been keeping you busy, I'm sure."

I glance toward Gabriel's office. He's on a conference call, door closed, privacy screen activated. I don't have a way to tell him that Cameron is here.

I have to set my pen down before I start clicking it furiously. "Mr. Reed is in a meeting. I can schedule you for later."

"Actually, I'm here to see you." Cameron sits in the chair across from my desk without invitation. "I have a proposition."

What the hell? My skin prickles with unease. "I'm sorry?"

"I need a new assistant, and I hear you have talents that are useful." His eyes move over me in a way that makes my stomach turn.

"I'm very happy in my current position," I say firmly. "Like, thrilled. And I'm learning so much. This is exactly where I want to be, so thanks but no thanks."

"Are you sure?" His eyes flick to my cleavage, lingering too long. "Because from what I hear, Gabriel can be quite controlling."

Mmm, controlling in the best of ways. I keep my expression neutral since this is not the time for inappropriate thoughts.

"Mr. Reed is an excellent boss."

"I'm sure he is. But wouldn't you like to explore your options? See what else is available?" He lowers his voice, leaning closer. "I could offer you opportunities Gabriel never could. Did you know I'm handling our clients in Singapore? Two months in Asia, first-class accommodations. You could see the world with me."

The way he says it makes my skin crawl. This isn't about a job offer. Cameron is trying to get to me to hurt Gabriel, and it's giving me major creepy vibes.

"As I said, I'm very happy here," I repeat.

"Just think about it. My offer is significantly more generous than whatever Gabriel's paying you. In every respect." Cameron stands and produces a business card like some evil magician. He places the card on my desk. "Call me when you're ready to broaden your horizons."

Right before he turns to leave, his eyes drop to my collar where my blouse has shifted, revealing a fading hickey. "I see Gabriel's marking his territory these days. How...primitive."

My blood runs cold, and I adjust my blouse. "I don't know what you're talking about."

"Sure, you don't." Cameron smiles coldly.

I don't say anything else as Cameron walks toward the elevator.

The moment the doors close behind him, Gabriel's office door opens. His eyes land on the business card on my desk.

"What did he want?" Gabriel's voice carries an edge.

I hold up the card. "Job offer. Though I'm pretty sure 'job' is a very loose interpretation of what he was actually offering."

Gabriel's jaw tightens. "Let's talk in my office."

I catch Jackie watching us curiously. Yeah, we shouldn't have this conversation in the open. I follow him into his office, and Gabriel closes the door. The privacy screen is still activated, so no one can see us.

"Tell me everything he said." Gabriel's voice is controlled but tight, like a wire about to snap.

I recount the conversation, watching Gabriel's expression darken with each detail. When I mention Cameron's comment about exploring options, Gabriel looks pissed.

"He knows what you mean to me, or thinks he knows," Gabriel says quietly.

How can Cameron know when I don't really know myself? "I'm not sure he does. You aren't exactly expressive in your affection."

"He knows because I'm treating you differently than I've ever treated an assistant or play partner before."

My stomach drops. "What does that mean for us?"

I see a flash of surprise in Gabriel's eyes. "Cameron can't change how I feel about you."

Again, I want to tell him he's never said how he really feels, but I'm afraid of his answer. I should just be happy with what I have with Gabriel.

"Everything out of Cameron's mouth is just him trying to make you doubt me."

"So, what're we going to do?"

Gabriel pulls me into his arms. "I'm going to do whatever I can to keep you deliriously happy so you're never tempted to take Cameron up on his offer."

Oh jeez, as if. I want to tell Gabriel to be serious, but I can feel the tension leaving his body so I decide to tease him.

"You know, Cameron saw the hickey you gave me."

"Oh, yeah?" He kisses my neck and sucks lightly. "Should I give you another one that is more visible."

"Hey!" I protest weakly and push him away.

Gabriel stops kissing me and moves to his desk to pick up a thick pen.

"What are you doing with that?"

Gabriel uncaps the pen. "I'm marking what's mine so there's no confusion."

He brushes my blouse aside, revealing the hickey, and writes something on my skin underneath it I can't see.

"What does it say?" I whisper.

"It's my initials. So everyone will know you're taken."

Holy fuck. He actually marked me. It's not permanent, but it's visible if my blouse shifts.

"Well, they'll know until it washes off," I joke.

He pulls me into his arms again and nibbles the other side of my neck before sucking harder, like he's really trying to leave another, more visible, hickey.

I laugh, and this time I'm firmer when I push him away. "You know, I still have to work here. I can't go out there waving my hickeys around like a tramp stamp."

"Fine. I have a better idea."

He moves to his desk, retrieving a long jeweler's box from the drawer. He opens it and holds out a delicate gold necklace. It's not the jewelry that makes my breath catch; it's the small pendant hanging from the chain. A lock.

"You bought that for me?" I whisper.

"Yes. I planned to talk to you about it before giving it to you, but now seems like a good time. It's a day collar. It would signify that you're mine."

"People would recognize what it is?"

"Some might, but no one would know for sure." He kisses my neck again. "Say you want to wear my collar."

"Gabriel," I breathe.

"Sir," he corrects, but his voice is gentle.

"Sir. Yes, I want to wear your collar."

He fastens the necklace, and I brush my fingers over it. I suddenly feel owned. It's odd what a piece of jewelry can do.

"Does this change anything?" I ask.

"Yes, it does." His hands frame my face. "Are you ready for a change?"

I meet his gaze, seeing my future reflected in his eyes.

"Yes, sir," I say. "I'm ready for anything."

Gabriel kisses me, and I taste possession, promise, and something that is dangerously close to love.

When we break apart, he rests his forehead against mine. "I'm not going to let Cameron ruin our happiness."

My heart squeezes joyfully. I make him happy.

CHAPTER 12

I'm reviewing a contract when my intercom buzzes. It's Jackie.

"Emergency. You're requested in Gabriel's office. Now."

I saw the senior partners go in there a bit ago, but I didn't think much of it. I grab my notepad and rush across the hall. Gabriel's door is closed, privacy screen activated, and I can hear raised voices through the soundproofing.

I knock once and enter without waiting for permission.

Gabriel stands behind his desk with barely controlled rage. Three senior partners sit across from him—Montgomery, Levine, and Park—their expressions grim. Cameron lounges in the corner chair, wearing a smug grin.

"Maya," Gabriel says, his voice carefully controlled. "Please sit."

The tension in the room is suffocating. I take the empty chair beside Gabriel's desk, clicking my pen nervously while trying to read the room. What's happening?

"Ms. Williams," Mr. Montgomery begins, "we need to discuss your relationship with Mr. Reed."

My stomach drops. "I'm sorry?"

Cameron produces a manila envelope from his briefcase. "These photographs were delivered to the senior partners this morning."

My blood turns to ice as Cameron slides photos across the desk. It's Gabriel and me entering his building together late at night, leaving together in the morning, his hand on my back in a way that suggests intimacy.

"The firm has strict policies about relationships between partners and staff," Ms. Levine says. "Particularly given the power differential."

Gabriel's hands clench into fists. "My personal life has no bearing on my work performance."

"Doesn't it?" Cameron interjects smoothly. "The Morrison deal nearly failed because of issues that arose after Ms. Williams began working closely with you. One might question whether personal entanglements affected your judgment."

That fucking snake. He's the one who tried to sabotage the Morrison deal, and now he's using it against us.

"The Morrison deal closed successfully," I say, finding my voice while my fingers twist the sleeve of my blouse nervously.

"After requiring all-night emergency sessions," Ms. Park observes. "Sessions where you and Mr. Reed were alone in the building for extended periods."

The implication hangs heavy in the air. My cheeks burn, but I force myself to maintain eye contact. I'm not ashamed of what we did in that library, but I'm not about to confirm it to these guys either.

"Ms. Williams," Mr. Montgomery continues, "we're prepared to offer you a generous severance package. Six months' salary, and excellent references."

"You're firing me?" I'm literally about to get fired for being a slut. My mom would be so proud.

"We're offering you an exit strategy," Cameron says, his voice dripping false concern. "Before this becomes a scandal that damages your career permanently."

Gabriel's control finally cracks. "This is bullshit."

"This is business," Mr. Montgomery replies coldly. "You have until the end of business today to resolve the situation."

The room falls silent except for the hum of the air conditioning. I can feel Gabriel's rage radiating from him like heat from a furnace.

"And if we refuse?" Gabriel asks.

"Then we'll be forced to call for a vote of no confidence," Ms. Levine says. "You built this firm, Gabriel, but you don't own it outright. The senior partners can remove you if necessary."

The threat hits like a physical blow. Gabriel built this firm back up after his father almost ruined it, and they're threatening to take it away because of me.

I look at Gabriel, and the fear and vulnerability in his steel-blue eyes makes my chest tight.

"I need to think about this," I say quietly.

Gabriel's jaw muscle ticks, but he nods. "Take all the time you need."

"Until five o'clock," Mr. Montgomery says. "The partners meet at five-fifteen to discuss next steps."

The meeting disperses with the solemnity of a funeral. The senior partners file out, followed by Cameron, who pauses at the door until they are out of earshot.

"There is another option," Cameron says. "Maya, my offer still stands. Work as my assistant, and the scandal dies down if you're no longer working directly under Gabriel."

This is it, the moment Cameron has been orchestrating. He wants to destroy Gabriel by taking me away, and he's given me a choice that feels like no choice at all.

His voice carries false sympathy. "I know this is difficult. But sometimes we have to make hard choices to protect the people we care about. Just think about it."

The moment the door closes behind Cameron, Gabriel's careful control shatters.

"Fuck!" He slams his palm against the desk. "Fifteen years building this firm, and they're ready to throw me out over photographs of us walking together."

"Gabriel..."

"I should have seen this coming. Cameron has been gathering evidence and waiting for the perfect moment." He turns to face me, and the pain in his eyes nearly breaks me. "I'm sorry, Maya. I'm so fucking sorry."

"Sorry for what?"

"For dragging you into this. For being selfish enough to pursue you when I knew Cameron wouldn't leave us alone."

I stand and move to him, placing my hands on his chest. "Stop. Just stop."

"You should take Cameron's offer," Gabriel says, his voice rough. "Your career is just beginning. Mine is already made."

"Are you serious right now?" My voice rises with anger. "You think I'm going to run to Cameron Webb because of some photographs? The guy who gives off serial killer vibes every time he looks at me?"

"Maya, be practical. If you stay as my assistant, no one will stop talking. Cameron is going to see to that. You deserve to grow and advance at the job without people assuming it's because you're sleeping with me."

"And what about us? What about what we have together?"

Gabriel's hands frame my face, his thumbs brushing my cheekbones. "What we have is the most important thing in my life. Which is exactly why I have to let you go."

The words hit me like a slap. "No."

"Maya—"

"No," I say more firmly. "I'm not some helpless assistant requiring a rescue. I'm not a victim in this story. I chose you, Gabriel. I chose this relationship, this dynamic. And I'm not walking away because some asshole thinks he can manipulate us."

Gabriel's eyes search mine. "What are you saying?"

"I'm saying fuck the senior partners, fuck their ultimatum, and especially fuck Cameron Webb." I step back, my mind racing. "You said you've been building a case against Cameron for weeks, right?"

"Yes. I've been quietly gathering evidence, but I didn't think I'd need it this soon."

"Well, you do!" My heart pounds so hard I can hear it in my ears. "Let's hit back with everything we've got."

I pull his laptop over to me, and my fingers fly over the keyboard. "Show me what you have so far."

Gabriel unlocks a password-protected folder on his computer. "After Cameron sent you those texts, I started reaching out to former employees who left abruptly. There's a pattern."

The files reveal what Gabriel's been collecting: testimonials from women who experienced Cameron's harassment, documentation of complaints that were buried, a timeline of suspicious employee transfers and departures.

"This is good," I say, scanning the evidence. "But we need more. You've got statements from Jessica and a few others, but we need current employees too. People who can speak to his ongoing behavior."

"That's the hard part," Gabriel admits. "No one wants to risk their career."

"But that's exactly what we're doing, isn't it?" I look up at him. "Maybe it's time others did too."

Gabriel studies my face for a long moment, then nods decisively. "What do you need?"

For the next four hours, we work with the intensity of two people fighting for their lives. Gabriel adds to his existing evidence while I reach out to current staff, carefully probing for information about Cameron's behavior.

The stories that emerge make my stomach churn. Unwanted advances disguised as mentorship. Threats of career sabotage for women who rejected him. A pattern of predatory behavior spanning years.

By 4:30, we have statements from six women, including Jessica, plus documentation of HR complaints that mysteriously disappeared and a detailed timeline of Cameron's escalating behavior.

"This could backfire if they think we're fabricating evidence in desperation," Gabriel warns as we prepare for the partners' meeting.

"Then we go down fighting. Together."

Gabriel's hand finds mine, squeezing gently. "I love you."

The words stop me cold.

"What?" I whisper.

"I love you, Maya Williams. I'm terrified of losing you, terrified of what loving you might cost both of us, but I can't pretend anymore that this is just about sex." His eyes hold mine. "I love your intelligence and your courage. I love the way you click that fucking pen when you're nervous."

My eyes fill with tears. "Gabriel..."

"I love you," he continues, "and I should have said it weeks ago."

"I love you, too." The words spill out.

Gabriel's mouth claims mine with desperate hunger, and I taste love and determination.

When we break apart, I straighten his tie and smooth his hair. "Ready to go save our future?"

"I'm ready for anything."

The conference room feels like a tribunal when we enter at exactly 5:15. The senior partners sit on one side of the table, Cameron on the other, all of them wearing expressions of grim determination.

"Ms. Williams," Mr. Montgomery begins, "have you reached a decision?"

"I have." I place a thick folder on the table, willing my hands not to shake. "We're filing formal harassment charges against Cameron."

The room erupts. Cameron shoots to his feet, his face flushing red. "This is ridiculous. You can't possibly—"

"Six women," I interrupt, my voice carrying the authority I've learned from Gabriel. "Six women are willing to testify about a pattern of sexual harassment, intimidation, and professional retaliation."

I open the folder, revealing statements, documented incidents, and evidence of Cameron's misconduct spanning years.

"Sarah Jenkins, contracts department. Violet Rodriguez, litigation. Amanda Foster, paralegal services. Jessica Pierce, former assistant." I meet each senior partner's eyes. "And two current employees who came forward this afternoon after learning about this meeting. There are probably more, but this is all we could get in a few hours to add to what Gabriel's been gathering for weeks."

Mr. Montgomery picks up the first statement, his expression growing darker as he reads. Ms. Levine and Ms. Park follow suit, the silence stretching as they absorb the evidence.

"This is fabricated," Cameron snarls. "Desperate lies from a woman trying to save her career."

"With sworn affidavits?" Gabriel asks mildly. "And people willing to give video testimony? Email evidence? If it's fabricated, Cameron, then you should have no problem with a full investigation."

"The firm has policies about workplace harassment," I continue, my voice steady. "Policies that protect employees from exactly this kind of predatory behavior. I'm demanding action."

Ms. Park looks up from the documents. "These are serious allegations."

"With serious evidence," Gabriel adds. "Evidence that's been accumulating for years while the firm turned a blind eye."

"Now wait just a minute—" Mr. Montgomery begins.

"No," I say firmly. "You wait. You called this meeting to force me out because of my relationship with Gabriel. A relationship between two consenting adults. Meanwhile, you've allowed Cameron Webb to harass women for years without consequence."

I feel the power of my convictions. "So here's my decision. I'm not taking the severance package. I'm staying here with Gabriel, and we're going to build a firm that protects its employees instead of protecting predators."

Cameron's control finally snaps. "You little bitch. You think you can destroy me with lies and manipulation?"

"I think I can destroy you with the truth," I reply calmly.

Gabriel smiles at me before addressing the other partners. "The question is whether this firm wants to be associated with Cameron Webb's behavior or with the kind of partnership Maya and I represent."

The senior partners exchange glances, silent communication passing between them.

Finally, Mr. Montgomery speaks. "We'll need time to review this evidence."

"Of course," Gabriel agrees. "You can take a full day like you gave us. But understand that if the firm protects Cameron, Maya and I will take our evidence, and my clients, elsewhere."

The loss of Gabriel's reputation and client relationships could devastate the firm if he leaves.

"This meeting is adjourned," Mr. Montgomery announces. "We'll reconvene tomorrow with our decision."

As we file out, Cameron grabs my arm. "This isn't over."

Gabriel moves like lightning, his hand clamping on Cameron's wrist. "Touch her again, and you'll regret it."

"Gentlemen," Mr. Montgomery barks. "Enough."

Cameron releases me, but his eyes promise retribution. "Enjoy your victory while it lasts."

Back in Gabriel's office, the adrenaline finally crashes. I sink into a chair, my legs feeling like jelly.

"Holy fuck," I breathe. "Did we just do that?"

Gabriel kneels beside my chair, taking my trembling hands. "You were incredible. Absolutely incredible."

"What if they choose him? What if we just destroyed our careers for nothing?" My mind races through worst-case scenarios. "I can barely afford my basement apartment. If I lose this job, I'll probably have to move back in with my roommate from college who had that weird collection of taxidermied rodents dressed as historical figures."

Gabriel's lips twitch at my rambling. "Then we start over." His voice carries absolute certainty. "What you did today—standing up to them and refusing to be intimidated—that's who you really are. Not my submissive assistant, but my equal partner."

I meet his eyes, seeing my future reflected there. "Partners in everything?"

"Everything," Gabriel confirms. "Business, pleasure, and whatever comes next."

A burst of delight pings through me. Even in this crisis, my body responds to him like it's hard-wired to his voice.

"So what now?" I ask, my fingers intertwining with his.

"Now we wait." Gabriel stands and pulls me to my feet. "And when we win tomorrow, I'm taking you home and showing you exactly what it means to be my partner in everything."

As he pulls me into his arms, I really feel like we're partners in every sense of the word.

And tomorrow, we'll find out if that's enough to save everything we've built.

CHAPTER 13

I pace Gabriel's office at 10 a.m. while we wait for the senior partners' decision. The coffee I poured an hour ago has gone cold, but my hands shake too much to drink it, anyway.

"They should have called by now," I mutter, checking my phone for the hundredth time. I can't stop moving. If I stop, I might throw up from the anxiety.

Gabriel sits behind his desk, outwardly calm, but I can see the tension in his jaw and that muscle ticking away like a time bomb.

"We gave them the entire day," he reminds me.

I click my pen rapidly. "What if they choose Cameron? What if they decide I'm not worth the trouble? What if you lose everything you've built because I wouldn't just take the stupid severance package?"

The intercom buzzes. It's Jackie.

"They're waiting for you in the conference room."

"Thanks, Jackie." Gabriel stands and takes my hand. "Ready?"

"No, but let's do this."

The mood in the conference room is different this morning. Less like a tribunal, more like a boardroom where actual business happens. Mr. Montgomery sits at the head of the table with Ms. Levine and Ms. Park flanking him. Cameron is notably absent, which could be good or catastrophically bad.

"Please sit," Mr. Montgomery says, his tone neutral.

We take our seats, and I touch my neck nervously, feeling Gabriel's collar beneath my blouse. Whatever happens, I'm his. That won't change.

Mr. Montgomery begins. "We've reviewed the evidence. All of it."

"Cameron has been terminated effective immediately," Ms. Park announces. "Security escorted him from the building this morning, and we're pursuing formal charges."

I bite my lip to keep from cheering. The relief hits me so hard I nearly slump in my chair.

"Furthermore," Ms. Levine continues, "we're implementing mandatory training for all partners and associates. Ms. Williams, your courage in coming forward has exposed serious deficiencies in our firm's culture."

Wait, they're actually thanking me? I was expecting to be fired or at least severely slut-shamed for fucking my boss.

"As for your relationship," Mr. Montgomery says, meeting our eyes directly, "we've concluded that two consenting adults conducting themselves professionally pose no threat to firm operations. Your work on the Morrison deal speaks for itself."

Gabriel's control finally cracks. "You're saying—"

"We're saying the firm values both of you too much to lose you over outdated moral panic," Mr. Montgomery replies with what might be a smile. "Though we recommend discretion in the workplace."

Like maybe don't fuck in the law library or under desks during conference calls? Seems fair.

"Thank you. All of you," I manage, my voice steadier than I feel.

Mr. Montgomery stands, indicating the meeting is over. "Cameron's client list will be redistributed. Several have specifically requested to work with your team."

As the partners file out, Gabriel turns to me with an expression of pure, unguarded pride. His mouth is on mine the moment the door closes.

When we break apart, he rests his forehead against mine. "Dinner tonight. Somewhere expensive. We're celebrating."

"Actually, I have other plans for celebrating."

His eyes darken with interest. "Such as?"

"Your penthouse. Your playroom. And a very thorough exploration of how it feels to be equals who choose our roles instead of being trapped in them."

"Maya—"

"Sir," I interrupt, grinning. "We're trying something different tonight."

"Different how?"

I lean close enough that my breath brushes his ear. "You'll see."

That evening, I stand in Gabriel's playroom wearing nothing but his collar and this new power humming under my skin. He leans against the doorframe, still fully suited, his eyes black with hunger. My pussy throbs just seeing him watch me like prey.

"Strip," I tell him.

Gabriel's eyebrows rise. "Excuse me?"

"You heard me. Take it all off. Now." I move to the wall of implements, selecting a silk flogger. "Tonight, I want to experience being in control."

For a moment, I think he'll refuse. Then his hands move to his tie, and I almost smile in triumph.

"Just tonight?" he asks.

Watching those long fingers unknot silk sends heat straight to my core. His jacket hits the floor. Then the shirt. My breathing becomes shallower with each button undone.

"Just tonight," I confirm. "Tomorrow, you can bend me over your desk again and make me come while I try to discuss cases. But right now, I want to explore."

My pussy buzzes with anticipation. I've never been on this side of the power dynamic before.

"Faster," I snap, running the ends of the flogger against my palm.

Gabriel obeys, kicking off his shoes, shoving pants and boxers down in one move. His cock springs free, already hard. My mouth waters, and I imagine sinking to my knees and sucking on him, but that's not happening. I have control.

"Bend over the bench." I smack the flogger against my palm and almost wince from the sting. "Ass up."

He moves without question, folding over the leather. Perfect. I run the flogger tails down his spine, watching goosebumps rise. "Tell me what you want."

"I want you to take what you need," he growls into the bench.

"Wrong answer." I bring the flogger down sharply across his ass. His muscles clench. "Try again."

His hips jerk. "Your pussy. I want your pussy wrapped around my cock."

Better. I strike the other cheek, harder this time. Pink blooms on his skin. "And?"

"I want to feel you come on me. Want to fill you up."

Good boy. I lay a flurry of quick strikes across his shoulders, ass, and thighs. I don't want to hurt him so I do it just enough to sting. Gabriel groans, pushing back into each hit. His cock bounces against the bench, leaking pre-cum. Fuck, I'm so wet I feel it trickling down my thigh.

"Up." I tap his hip with the flogger handle. "Bed. On your back."

He moves quickly, eyes locked on mine. I climb over him, straddling his hips with his cock in front of me.

"Hands on the headboard," I order. "Don't move them."

Gabriel obeys, gripping the metal bars. His chest heaves. I slide up his body, my pussy dragging along his shaft. So fucking thick. I pause with his tip just nudging my entrance.

"Beg," I whisper.

"Please." His knuckles go white on the bars. "I need to be inside you."

I sink down slowly, stretching around him inch by inch. "God, you're huge," I gasp when he's fully seated.

His hips buck, and I clamp my thighs tightly, squeezing his cock until he stops moving.

"Hold still. It's my turn." I ride him with slow rolls at first, grinding deep.

Sweat beads on his temples, and his jaw clenches. "You know I want to toss you over and fuck you hard, right?"

Yeah, I know he's just playing at being submissive for me, but this is fun.

"Shut up. You're my fucktoy tonight, and fucktoys have to just lay there and take it." I pick up speed, bouncing now, taking him deep with every drop. "Gonna milk you dry."

His abs flex under my hands. "Christ."

"Gonna make you come inside me." I slam down hard, making us both gasp. "Gonna make you breed me. Pump me full."

He bucks hard, almost throwing me off. "Say it again."

"Breed me." I ride him faster, impaling myself over and over. "Fill my pussy with your cum. Make it drip out of me."

Gabriel's control snaps. His hands leave the headboard, grabbing my hips to slam me down harder. "Come for me. Now."

Ordering me even now? Fuck, it works. My pussy clenches hard around his cock. "Oh God, yes!"

Pleasure explodes, wringing his cock as I scream. Gabriel roars, thrusting up deep as he pulses inside me. Hot. Thick. Claiming.

I collapse on his chest, both of us panting. His cum leaks out around his still-hard cock. He's mine. All mine.

"That was incredible," I admit. "But..."

"But?" Gabriel's arms tighten around me.

"I still prefer you in charge," I mumble. My legs feel like jelly, and my mind is blissfully quiet. "I like being your good girl too much."

Gabriel grins. "Even after tonight?"

"Especially after tonight. Because I know I choose it. Every time."

Gabriel flips me onto my back, looming over me. "Good. Because I'm never letting you go."

His mouth slants across mine, and I melt into familiar submission.

"I have something for you," Gabriel says, reaching for the nightstand. He produces a small velvet box, and my breath catches. Holy fuck. Is this what I think it is?

"Gabriel..."

"Marry me," he says simply. "Not because you're my submissive. Marry me because you're my partner in everything."

I stare at the beautiful solitaire ring that somehow perfectly matches the collar around my neck. Just a few months ago, I was serving coffee and a struggling student. Now I'm being proposed to by the most brilliant man I've ever met.

"Yes," I whisper, my voice cracking. "Yes, to everything."

As Gabriel slides the ring onto my finger, I realize this is what happily ever after looks like. It's not perfect people finding each other but flawed people choosing to build something beautiful together.

"Mrs. Reed," Gabriel murmurs against my lips.

"Mmm, I like the sound of that."

I gasp as he slides his cock inside me, fucking me slowly. There's no doubt in my mind that this is the man I want to spend the rest of my life with.

Epilogue

A year later...

I straighten up from the toilet, wiping my mouth with the back of my hand and staring at the blue line on the pregnancy test. It's positive.

My stomach flips with excitement at the thought of telling Gabriel. Six months of marriage, and the only thing that's changed is that I now wake up to his face every morning instead of in my shitty basement apartment. Well, that and the fact that I'm now Maya Reed, though I use Williams professionally.

I hide the test in my pocket when I hear the elevator ding. We've been officially trying for two months, ever since he whispered, "It's time to put a baby in you," while fucking me against the window of our bedroom. The image of him coming inside me while overlooking the city skyline still makes my thighs clench.

"Maya?" His voice carries through our penthouse.

"In here!" I call out and quickly rinse my mouth with mouthwash. Morning sickness is a bitch, but at least now I know why I've been puking for the past week.

Gabriel appears in the doorway, loosening his tie. Even after six months of marriage, the sight of him still makes my heart skip. He's in a black suit today, looking every inch the powerful attorney who makes million-dollar deals before lunch.

"You're home early," I say, trying to act normal.

His eyes narrow slightly. "You're pale. Are you sick again?"

I bite my lip, suddenly nervous. We've fucked like rabbits to make it happen, but now that it's real, I'm terrified he might not be ready.

"I have something to tell you," I say, fidgeting with the sleeve of my blouse.

Gabriel steps closer, concern replacing suspicion. "What's wrong?"

I pull the test from my pocket and hold it up. "I'm pregnant."

For a moment, he just stares, his face unreadable. Then a flash of raw emotion in his eyes makes my breathe catch.

"You're sure?" he asks roughly.

I nod. "The test is positive."

He crushes me against him, kissing me so fiercely it makes my knees weak. His hands frame my face, and when he pulls back, he looks at me with awe.

"You're carrying my child," he says, and it's not a question but a statement of possession that lights my entire body up with joy.

"Yeah," I breathe. "Looks like it finally stuck."

He laugh, that full laugh I love, and drops to his knees in front of me. His hands slide under my shirt to rest on my still-flat stomach.

"Our baby," he murmurs. "Growing inside you."

Holy fuck, his reverence is hot. My body responds instantly, nipples tightening as heat pools between my legs. This might just be pregnancy hormones, but honestly, this is how I always feel around him.

"I guess all that breeding worked," I tease, running my fingers through his hair.

His eyes darken. "I've been very thorough."

That's an understatement. Ever since we decided to try for a baby, Gabriel's dominance has taken on a new primal and possessive edge that focused entirely on filling me with his cum. The word "breed" has become a trigger that makes my pussy flutter every time he growls it against my skin.

He stands and lifts me onto the bathroom counter. "We should celebrate."

"Here? Now?" I laugh, even as my legs part instinctively.

"Right fucking here. Right fucking now."

He pushes my skirt up around my waist, and my head spins as he tears my panties off with a sharp rip.

"Those were expensive," I protest weakly.

"I'll buy you more," he growls, freeing his cock from his pants. "Spread your legs wider."

I obey instantly, my body responding to his commands on autopilot. I'm still his submissive in private.

"You're soaked," he observes, fingers sliding through my folds. "Does carrying my baby turn you on?"

"Everything about you turns me on," I gasp as he circles my clit. "You know that."

"Tell me," he commands, positioning himself at my entrance.

"I love being pregnant with your baby."

He slides into me, and I cry out in pleasure.

"Mine," he growls, fucking me hard enough that I have to grip the edge of the counter for support. "All fucking mine."

"Yes," I gasp, head falling back as pleasure builds rapidly. "Yours, sir. Always yours."

His hand rests on my lower belly while he fucks me. "I'm going to fuck you every day," Gabriel promises, his voice rough with need. "Keep you full of my cum even though you're already pregnant. Would you like that?"

"Yes, sir," I moan as his cock hits that perfect spot inside me. "Please."

"Such a good girl," he praises, and those words still make me melt. "My ring is on your finger, my collar around your neck, and now my child is growing inside you."

My orgasm builds with shocking speed, coiling tightly at the base of my spine. "Oh God, I'm going to come!"

"Squeeze my cock while you think about how I'm going to keep breeding you over and over again. I might just keep you knocked up and pregnant for the rest of your life."

God, why does that sound appealing? The orgasm hits me like a tidal wave, intense and overwhelming. I convulse around him, crying out as pleasure radiates through every nerve ending. Gabriel follows immediately, his release triggered by my pulsing walls. He grunts, burying himself deep as he fills me with cum.

As we come down, breathing hard against each other, my phone dings from the counter beside us. I reach for it while Gabriel kisses my neck, still inside me.

It's an email from Jessica Pierce. I scan it quickly, then look up at Gabriel.

He catches my expression. "What?"

"It's from Jessica." I hold up the phone so he can read it too:

Thought you'd want to know that Cameron Webb accepted a plea bargain. Two years with the possibility of parole in fourteen months for blackmail and witness intimidation. Eight more women came forward after your case. Thank you for your courage.

"Two years," I murmur. "That doesn't seem like enough."

Gabriel's jaw tightens, but there's satisfaction in his eyes. "It's not about the time. It's about the fact that he'll never practice law again. Never hold power over women again."

I lean into his chest, suddenly emotional. "We did that. We stopped him."

"You did that," Gabriel corrects, tucking a strand of hair behind my ear. "Your courage. Your strength."

"Our partnership," I insist. "I wouldn't have done it without you backing me."

He smiles that genuine smile that still makes my heart flutter. "Partners in everything."

"Speaking of partnerships," I say, sliding off the counter and straightening my skirt, "how do you feel about a nursery in the spare bedroom? I was thinking maybe that space next to your playroom?"

Gabriel's eyes darken with interest. "Convenient arrangement."

I laugh, knowing exactly what he's thinking. "For when the baby's asleep and we need adult time?"

"Precisely." He tucks himself back into his pants and adjusts his tie. "Though we should probably soundproof the playroom more thoroughly."

My pussy throbs at the thought of all the noise we've made in there. Yeah, it definitely needs more soundproofing.

"I can't believe we're doing this," I admit, touching my stomach. "A year ago, I was serving coffee and worrying about my electric bill. Now I have a wonderful career, I'm married to the hottest man in New York, and I'm pregnant with his baby."

Gabriel pulls me against him. "Any regrets?"

"Not a single one," I say honestly. "Except maybe that we didn't fuck in the library more often before it was suggested that we stop."

He laughs against my hair. "Who says we can't still do that? We'll just have to be quieter."

My body hums at the suggestion. "You're a bad influence, you know that?"

"Says the woman who sucked my cock under my desk during a conference call."

"Fair point."

As I look up at my husband, I feel a sense of completeness I never thought possible. This man, who dominates me in private and supports me in public, helped me find a strength I never knew I had.

"I love you," I say simply.

"I love you too," Gabriel replies, his hand resting protectively on my stomach. "Both of you."

And holy fuck, I can't wait to see where this wild ride takes us next.

The End

ABOUT APRIL CROSS

I'm a writer of spicy stories...okay, I'll be honest, most of my stuff is ghost pepper spicy. I started writing wife sharing stories under Lacey Cross before branching out to longer romantic erotica. I write power play stories with guys who demand to be in control.

www.ingramcontent.com/pod-product-compliance
Lightning Source LLC
Chambersburg PA
CBHW020810310726
48969CB00002B/789